Praise for *Only Everything*

Tragic, triumphant, and at times painfully self-disclosing, *Only Everything* beckons us into a world which, once there, we realize is actually our own. Martin-Smith knowingly and lovingly kicks the rust off long-forgotten passion and questions whose urgency we'd often rather forget: What makes art stay? Can love and art exist without each other? What's worth risking for the life you'd die to live?

Through meticulous observation and magnanimous narration, *Only Everything* reminds even the most cynical postmodernist what great fiction can do: reveal downright existential truths in the subtlest gesture. In this way — and countless others — Martin-Smith's exploration of the American Dream's more disheveled and melancholy cousin, the Artist's Dream, illuminates the humble, heartbreaking path of transformation.
— Angela Raines, writer, consultant, and collaborator on the award-winning *The Art of Money*

All of us long to unwind one of life's grandest riddles: to realize our dreams but never fully exhaust them, to taste their sweetness but not lose our appetite — a riddle that lives at the intersection of being and becoming, of love and loss, of art and ordinary, of regret and hope.

Keith Martin-Smith has given us a rare gift of literary honesty, a treasure box of a story where dreams are the hidden character on every page, inside a man who hasn't earned the life he wants because he hasn't yet accepted the life he has. Someone who, like each of us, has to learn to find himself well beyond the ephemeral dream. With dazzling insight and masterful prose, Martin-Smith takes us deep into the riddle of the human life, and we emerge far better for it.
— Robb Smith, CEO Integral Life

Only Everything is raw, riveting, and relatable. It's heartachingly real, full of understated empathy. What Martin-Smith leaves unsaid packs the strongest punch. The interwoven story lines leave a lasting impression, an indelible imprint on the heart and psyche. From the banalities of the corporate work machine to the devastating effects of random brutality ... and the hindsight that provokes yet leaves no room for mercy.

It will appeal to anyone who grapples with blind spots about their numbing job, tumultuous past, or unfinished love stories. I can't recommend this read highly enough; you will not be able to put it down. It arcs from gut-wrenching loss to quiet redemption in the unexpected. An insistent humanity shines through the darkness of protagonist Logan's winding journey, from the promise and pitfalls of his urban youth to the seasoned, hard-earned wisdom of middle age in the Rocky Mountains.

It's a wonder what the human heart can withstand in terms of loss and damage, but more wondrous still the highlights Martin-Smith captures in his aptly capable way. Uncompromising in its brutal truth and beauty, if *Only Everything* doesn't crack your heart open, you ought to consider seeing either a shrink or a shaman.

Don't fail to read this gripping autobiographical novel. It will stay with you long after you've turned the last page.
— Sarah C. Beasley, author and columnist, *Buddhist Door*

Now more than ever we're challenging what it means to be a man. We're challenging our career and relationship choices, power, sexuality, and our fantasies around success — everything that impacts the way we experience life. But when we tear down the stories that gave our lives comfort, we can get lost in the uncertainty. And maybe that's the thing we fear the most. *Only Everything* is the story of one man's journey to

tear down the limiting beliefs and bullshit from the inside out. We get to join him on the ride as each layer of himself is ripped away. I'd suggest you wear a helmet.
— Tripp Lanier, host of the *New Man* podcast

In a time filled with New Age spiritual pundits vehemently presenting lies about the way reality works, as if their declarations were obvious universal truths, *Only Everything* is a welcome respite. The book boldly counters the delusion that being more of something guarantees a certain outcome.

In this original novel, the reader takes a journey through one artist's life as he is reminded of a much more grounded and salt-of-the-earth truth about "ordinary" folks. And how sometimes, when we work really hard and do the right thing, we end up working really hard and doing the right thing. The reader is left to decide if facing this truth is a form of giving up or growing up.
— Sarah Marshank, author of *Being Selfish: My Journey from Escort to Monk to Grandmother*

Only Everything is a beautifully written story about a writer's journey, told with unvarnished truth about the stakes, the struggles, and the sacrifice that come with the impulse to bring something larger than yourself into the world.
— Ross Hostetter, author of *Keepers of the Field*

Only Everything

keith martin-smith

Perception Press

Denver • Philadelphia • New York

Only Everything

Published by Perception Press, 2018
www.perceptionpress.org

Edited by Kathryn Thomas
Cover concept by Alyssa Morin
Cover design and typesetting by BookCoverCafe.com

Print ISBN: 978-0-692-11600-5
eBook ISBN: 978-0-692-13150-3

Acknowledgements

Many friends, family members, and colleagues had a hand in helping this book take shape. I especially want to note those who backed a successful Kickstarter campaign I ran that allowed me to focus on the creation of this book. Hundreds of people were very generous in their support, but Jon Brandon, Robert P. Schmidt Jr., Ali Shanti, and Laura Emlen went above and beyond.

I also want to thank Madeleine Marx, Robert McNaughton, Marco Lam, and Melody Blackis for vital and critical feedback on early drafts of this novel.

For Alyssa

If my dreams stood before me as years, I would live forever.

Monday

The sun rises rude and intense and disregarding of the headache that presses dully with each heartbeat. I try to hide my face in the pillow but without the blinds drawn it is like trying to stay dry under a waterfall. I surrender and go through the routine: coffee, shower, clothes sticking to a wet back. I pause to look at myself in the bathroom mirror. Through the steam hazing my image I see a man older than I remember, bruised under eyes dark and veiled with sleep, jaw set in a hard line. The mirror-man used to smile sometimes, sometimes growl, sometimes look playfully back, but more and more he looks like this man, tired and aging.

Before I leave I go in to kiss her. She is awake.

"I'm off to work," I say. "I hope you have a good day."

"You too," she replies, throwing off the covers. "Can you put the kettle on before you leave?"

A nod and a trip down the stairs, kettle switched on, followed by the long drive to work, NPR talking in energetic voices about the emerging news of the day.

The office is open-plan, intended to imply equality with the executives working next to the office managers and junior sales associates. It certainly gives that impression — so long as one doesn't compare paystubs or the gender of the leadership. It's a tech startup, the kind of company that has transformed my home on the Front Range of Colorado from a once-sleepy mountain town full of hippies and cowboys into a hipster and Tesla-filled upwardly mobile, increasingly crowded region.

My position is in marketing, that slippery first cousin of advertising. I'm the Content Marketing Manager, a fancy way to say I get paid to write stuff that drives customers into the wide end of a marketing funnel, not unlike the giant fishing nets cast by professional fisherman to catch as many fish as possible, never mind the occasional drowned dolphin or sea turtle.

I nod at my team, take my seat, open my laptop, and stare at it blankly. It's Monday and we have our weekly marketing meeting at 9:30. I pass forty-five minutes in an under-caffeinated crawl of work until we are finally summoned into the large modernist conference room dubbed Rectangle. Clever — as the room is, in fact, rectangular.

We take seats around the table, a beautiful single cut of exotic wood with slivers of glass through the middle. My boss, Steve, is eight years younger than me. He's an executive vice president, or EVP, which means he's very ambitious and very good at his job, since most EVPs are in their forties or fifties. He's a youthful-looking man prone to wearing tucked-in checkered shirts with designer skinny jeans squeezed over heavy legs. He wears that universal badge of hipsterhood, the groomed beard, on his oval face. He gets his hair cut every two weeks so it never changes in its perfect, gel-infused, breaking blonde wave.

Steve has the California habit of ending every third or fourth sentence on an up-note, making his statements sound strangely like questions.

He is speaking. With effort I pay attention. "So the thing is, when we look at inbound marketing streams and how they impact the bottom line, we need to look for metrics, of course. How do we measure marketing success, right? We haven't done a good job of that yet — we've been understaffed, which isn't an excuse — but now we have the right team in place and so we can put those metrics in place to see what kinds of impacts we're having before an inbound lead gets handed off to a BDR on the way to becoming an MQL, and our results from last quarter stand up pretty well — I'm glad we have Jamie now to handle this better than I could? So we're in good shape, but we can do better, right? So for today, let's go around and talk about where you are in supporting this quarter's MQLs and SQLs, with the purpose of making sure we're not getting too siloed in our roles but are working in ways that are making the team operate as one. Not that we don't have our own projects. But I'm concerned that our silos — our swim lanes — are too narrowly focused? So while Logan is mainly in charge of MQLs, Jen really takes over halfway through the sales cycle, converts them into SQLs for the BDRs, and Jamie tracks our ROI and engagement along the way so we can track our success — not that it's always trackable week to week — so we can dynamically steer marketing? We have some big projects coming up in Q2. Let's start with Logan and get everything onto the table."

I clear my throat. Fucking marketing acronyms. BDRs. SQLs. MQLs. RFPs. CPCs. CRs. ROIs. USPs. They are endless. In most meetings, half a dozen get dropped. I say my bit for the meeting. With some modesty I can say that I'm a good writer. My job is largely about writing. But when it comes to fitting into a company culture, in presenting things inside the accepted silos of communication, in working as part of a team, and in caring about a corporate mission, I'm afraid my experience is as lacking as my heart. Yet here I am speaking with relative competence about a piece of paid content I am creating for the company to generate more emails for our list and to get more people interested in an upcoming webinar. All stuff that generates MQLs, or *market qualified leads* — which can, in turn, lead to five- or six-figure accounts for the company.

Jamie is a young Korean woman who joined the company after me. As sharp and fast as a guillotine, her intense drive is filtered through often-dismissive Millennial sarcasm. I'm a little scared of her.

"Uh," she says, a finger twirling around a long strand of black hair, curled at the ends. Her eyes roll from her computer to me, without any movement of her head. "So, like, you're going to write that up this week?" I know, somehow, she went to Oral Roberts University, which makes her and me not just different kinds of people but a different species altogether.

I nod. Jamie is wearing black thigh-high socks and a blue skirt. When she sits and crosses her legs as she is doing now, there is a four-inch gap of skin I try not to notice. An off-white blouse drapes each shoulder and is secured up to the modest second-to-last button. A gold cross hangs from her neck just above the unseen chasm of her cleavage.

"So, uh, are you, like, setting up metrics to track the inward bound traffic to see where people are coming from when they get to the paper?" She puts on a pair of designer glasses with angled black frames.

I look around the table. Jen, another young colleague, blonde and blue eyed and recently a mother, is staring hard at her computer screen. Steve is looking at me, a groomed eyebrow raised in anticipation. I'm a relatively new hire, after all, and one he made, so my competence is a direct reflection on him.

"Well," I say, stalling and thinking, "yes." I pause. I then make a tactical decision to not bullshit, because I'm pretty sure I'll get busted. "But I could use a little help in getting that set up."

"Good," Steve says quickly. "Jamie, can you help Logan with that?"

She sighs and there is the tiniest roll of her eyes. "Of course." My hand reflexively goes to my neck.

"Okay," Steve says, "thanks, Logan. Jen, do you want to walk us through where you are in supporting the BDRs?"

I exhale.

Fall, 1995

The East Village was a different New York in those days. You've heard the stories, usually tinged with nostalgia, an irritant to anyone who spent time in a city that was dirty, dangerous, expensive, and yes, glorious. It was like a geologic phenomenon where two great pressure plates were converging into a single stress fracture known as Avenue A. I had a two hundred square foot apartment on the front lines of that stress point. It was more expensive than I could afford but it was in Manhattan and it was all mine.

The bulk of Alphabet City — Avenues A through D — belonged to its long time residents, mostly poor Puerto Rican and African American families who had called that area home for a generation. The neighborhood was punctuated with graffiti and vacant lots, and most weekends saw its corners full of young men openly selling and using drugs. Not surprisingly, there was little reason for nonresidents to go there except to score a dime bag or a little blow, for the check cashing and loan businesses, heavily gated bodegas where men worked behind two inches of smeared Plexiglas, and interchangeably filthy Chinese food storefronts offered little value to them. Alphabet City averaged five thousand major crimes a year, all by itself, from rape to murder to robbery.

Avenue A marked the porous line between two worlds, proudly punk and bohemian on one side and poor and desperate on the other. Those trying to make art and live outside the constraints of the dominant culture were stacked next to those trying to survive inside it.

I hopped down the gum-stained, dog-piss-covered steps to the sidewalk, bag slung over my shoulder. It was early fall. I had been in the city only for a few weeks. Five months out of university and I was on my way to the first real interview of my life. I checked my watch, a cheap metal Seiko with a scratched face, and realized I had time to kill. I turned into a Catholic Church. I was born Catholic but had become contemptuous of that religion. Still, the shadow of the church was a long one: I considered myself an *ex*-Catholic, a term that implied divorce over indifference.

I walked through the vestibule and into the sanctuary. It resembled most older churches in the city, the stained glass spreading moody blues and reds across the pews. I took an uncomfortable seat halfway to the altar, letting my eyes wander through the space, taking in the familiar sights and smells. Stale frankincense was in the air from the morning's service, its velvety and musky smell the olfactory archetype of my childhood. There was only a muffled hint of the flowing city a hundred feet behind me. An emaciated Christ hung in front of me, cheekbones hollowed and eye sockets pronounced. This was the cliché of my school years, a torn and defeated man reproduced in every classroom with a fetishist's level of detail.

My interview was for a full time job in publishing as a low-level editor. I'd gone to college and gotten my degree, moved to a place where there was opportunity, and was now working my way into the adult world.

So why did it feel wrong?

My family history was one where neither grandfather had made it to high school. My own father had been raised in the Depression-era south, in a world where the biggest dreams were of food on the table and the freedom of owning a car. He'd managed to ride out of the rural South to a full college scholarship on the post-war boom, the first and only one in his family to do so. Growing up I viewed jobs as sacred and money as more precious than faith.

I considered. I knew I loved to write and always had. Bad stories and worse writing, sure, but writing nonetheless. That feeling of carving a character out of nothing but little ink marks on a page thrilled me with its power and promise. Writing was what I wanted to do, and I'd figured that a job in publishing was close to a writer's life. But I now realized in a moment of insight it wasn't. It was more like being a roadie than a musician — close to the dream and a world away from it.

I thought of Franklin, my older brother. He was a professional illustrator and on-the-cusp-of-fame fine artist who also lived in the city and had been pushing his way into the art world for half a decade. He showed me that it was possible, if incredibly difficult, to follow the artist's path, even though he seemed inexplicably and unattainably more extroverted, handsome, cocksure, and talented. For me, the darker and quieter brother, a full time job seemed a more reasonable and safe prospect from which I might step forward into the world. Still, if I took this job, I might feel closer to coming out of the gates with my legs bound.

I looked at my watch: 11:15. I would need to head toward the subway now to be on time for the interview. I shifted. I had a formidable work ethic instilled from my Catholic upbringing. Some talent, according to a creative writing professor. A couple of finished short stories. The passion to write. A sense that I was, somehow, meant to be different from those around me, an idea instilled so perniciously and so discreetly it was like the seed of a great, undetectable cancer: if I followed my passion, life would have no choice but to open itself up to me. Hard work and talent, tempered with sacrifice, could only led to success.

One of the three other people in the church, a middle-aged Hispanic woman with a square, serious face, stood and crossed herself, shuffling down the aisle with a lowered head.

I stood. I saw two distinct paths, two mutually exclusive ways of being — awake or asleep, drunk or sober, alive or dead. One path was the security of a job with benefits and a pension plan. The other was the path of struggle where I might develop experiences outside the security of full time work, live in the fire of a life without a safety net, and actually have something to write *about*. I didn't want to be the forty-year-old still trying to write his first novel, still clinging to some idea that he might, one day, break free of the prison of his own life. This wasn't going to be a hobby, a creative middling to make the suck of a full time job more palatable. I saw an all-in wager: write while living insecurely but fully, wildly, freely, on my own terms and no one else's, the Flying fucking Wallendas without the net.

A moment later I pushed through the doors, raising a hand to shield my eyes from the light. I looked left, toward the subway, and right, toward my apartment. Adjusting the bag on my shoulder, I turned right.

Monday Night

I'm on top. Between us is a fine layer of sweat. She is wet. She is always wet, in a way that makes my desire uncoil and want to explode out of me. I change position, hooking my hands in the hinge of her knees and pushing them back. Our eyes meet before I let mine go slightly out of focus, leaning harder on the inside of her knees. There is resistance, almost imperceptible. A subtle pushback, a slight refusal, so small I'm not sure I feel it. I pause and unhook my hands, settling onto her body, less threatening, less invasive, pushing my desire back down a notch. I still feel the pressure of her legs against me, her inner thighs resisting me in a way that subtly subdues me.

In the beginning things had been different between us, more passionate, more reckless. Sex on tables and in bathrooms and on office desks. But that's the way things always are in the beginning, and in youth. I tell myself it's just the passage of time, the march into early middle age that slowly turns fucking into lovemaking.

Her eyes find mine and linger, maybe looking for something and not finding it, for we don't manage to connect there and she looks away. I arrange my body in the way I know brings her to climax, guiding her legs into a place where she'll be able to relax. She does, then so do I. A few moments later her breath deepens and she grabs at my back, moaning softly as I orgasm. I look down at her body in the half light, my cum in a neat line from solar plexus to the base of her throat. Exhaustion rushes in to fill the void where arousal had been, so fast that for a moment it's hard to support my own weight. The desire to fuck is replaced with the desire for oblivion.

"Tissues?" Her eyes indicate the left side of the bed.

I lean through my haze and grab at the box, needing two swipes before catching a tissue and then studiously wiping her clean. We both get out of bed, her into pajamas and me into jeans and a button-down shirt.

"Tomorrow's *such* a full day," she sighs. "My God. It's full of phone meetings and planning for the next quarter."

"How many meetings?" Disconnection and a vague frustration arise like mild indigestion.

"Five," she says. "First meeting is at eight. Then four more. I have to get some sleep."

"Well," I say automatically, "I hope you sleep well."

"Sweet of you," she replies, sticking a toothbrush between her teeth. She pulls socks over her bare feet, the toothbrush hanging from a corner of her mouth. A minute later she's in bed, a book opened. I kiss her.

"Would you mind sleeping in the other room," she asks. I look over our king-sized bed with its full pillows and thick down comforter. "It's just ... if you come in a couple of hours from now and wake me up, I won't be able to fall back asleep. Or if you snore." She pauses. "Or drink too much. It makes you smell. Tomorrow is going to be long enough as it is."

"Okay." I swallow against the indigestion.

I close the door and go downstairs, pouring a whiskey. Cask conditioned. Refined. Local. The batch number is even written on the bottle: #327. I look around the house. It's modern and adult, not like the half-furnished and run-down places that populated so much of my twenties and thirties. Hardwood floors, granite countertops, new windows, furniture with matching pillows and blankets, a couch that doesn't attempt to eat you when you sit down or steal the change from your pockets. It is all very nice, indicating that we have arrived into adulthood and can afford to spend money on design instead of just on function. I swallow the whiskey; its gentle bite is reassuring, like a warm hand on my shoulder.

Three drinks later it's finally tolerable to be in my own body. The stress in my shoulders and low back, warmed from within, begins to release. Everything, in fact, seems softer and easier, the TV more reassuring in its self-importance, the darkness of the night an invitation to rest.

I climb the stairs and into the small, uncomfortable bed in my study. As I turn on my side, a ghostly white fiber arises from my sacrum, a poisonous vapor of nervousness wrapping itself around my heart. At the same time, I realize the depth of my crushing fatigue. I ignore one while embracing the other, and for the next hour try and force what will only respond to surrender. Finally, defeated, I sit up and place my bare feet onto the hardwood floor. I try sitting on the meditation cushion I keep in my study, but a few minutes there is like a few minutes in a boxing ring. Dazed, I stand and kick the cushion back into the corner with a mumbled curse.

Back downstairs I open another bottle of whiskey and smile at the sound as the cork slides from the neck. I bring my nose down close and breathe deeply. The white coils of anxiety have risen to my head; my thoughts turn and circle back on themselves in neurotic loops. I walk the length of the house once and back, twice and back, ice chinking in the glass I'm holding. I know these kinds of nights, where the quiet and the dark act like a magnifying glass on all that's warped and cracked inside. And I know the way out. I drink, and I pace, and after three more glasses I fall through the back door of my mind. I settle onto the couch and into an uneven sleep, and when the early dawn wakes me the anxiety is gone, replaced with the dull throb of a headache.

Fall, 1995

I think you should go for it," Carissa said, looking at me with green eyes set in a swath of freckles starting at each ear and reaching their crescendo across the bridge of her nose. "But I don't think it's going to be easy."

She put her hand over her mouth and laughed through it when she saw my response. "Aw, *baby*! That doesn't mean it's going to be *hard*!" She leaned forward and kissed me on the forehead.

I laughed as well, but with more embarrassment than humor. "You don't think it's ridiculous? That *I'm* ridiculous?"

"Of course you are," she laughs. "That's why I love you. When does an artist decide they want to be a writer or painter or whatever? You can do anything if you put your mind to it, right? And you have to make the choice at *some* point. If you're going to work through your first novel or painting, you have to believe in yourself, don't you?"

"I guess."

"You *guess*? You just told me so! And I quote — " Her voice dropped into a mock baritone. "'Now's as good a time as any. I'm at a crossroads and choosing a path.'"

"Fuck you," I laughed, pinching her and making her yelp. We'd been dating since our junior year in college, or rather my junior year. Carissa was never really organized enough to be in any particular year of school. When I graduated, she'd figured she'd had about enough of her formal education and followed me to New York City.

We were sitting in her bedroom in Manhattan, a one-bedroom flat above Third Avenue and Twenty-Second, easy walking distance to a dozen fantastic neighborhoods. It was far from a perfect place, but in those days comfort could always take a backseat to access.

13

The hardwood floors, exposed brick, and high ceilings made it feel bigger and nicer than it actually was. Third Avenue, right outside the windows, was a loud and inconsiderate neighbor who belched exhaust, screeched brakes, blew horns at all hours of the day and night, and played a combination of base-thumping rock and roll, rap, and R&B — sometimes all at the same time.

Amy was Carissa's roommate. Her space was denoted by a sliding purple curtain that could be drawn across the entire main room, cutting off her two-thirds. Her side consisted of the two large windows, a bunk bed with a rumpled futon under it, an off-white drafting table whose bent leg and scored surface made it a likely dumpster find, and a host of wilting plants in various stages of distress. On the shared side of the purple-curtained divide were a three-person kitchen table, a four-by-four kitchenette, and the apartment's only bathroom.

I opened an oversized bottle of red wine and poured two glasses. It was a fall night and the heat of the day came in through the windows along with the smell of exhaust, occasional shouts, the staccato blare of cop cars and first responders, and the impatient horns of cabbies blowing the moment a light changed from red to green.

We sat on her corner loveseat in a room crowded with a queen bed and black Ikea-made entertainment hutch that doubled as a closet and storage rack. The walls were decorated in a post-college menagerie of posters. A strand of Christmas lights secured with thumbtacks lit one wall.

"It just seems very self-serious," I said, pressing the point.

"Choosing to be a writer?"

"Yeah." An especially loud delivery truck, sounding as if it were about to rattle itself to pieces, clattered past.

Carissa was, as my grandmother might say, no bigger than a minute. She stood just over five feet tall and had a tiny circular face that made her seem younger than her twenty-one years. Her hair was shoulder-length and brown, but she was taken to trying different ways to color it. At that moment it was, from her ears down, white-blonde. Her eyes were my favorite part of her face, green and bright. She had no real chin to speak of, a dot of a nose, and tiny ears. She liked to dress in clothes that were too big for her; she always seemed to swim inside of overalls, baggy jeans, or large sweaters.

As the truck's interruption faded up Third Avenue, I continued. "I'm aware that the reach of my ambition is greater than my talent. I guess I have to live with that." I looked out the window.

"See, Logan? That's a very writerly thing to say."

"Are you sure? Maybe this how they define arrogance."

"No, baby, it's how they define narcissism."

We both laughed.

"He felt destined," Carissa said, sitting up and thrusting her small chest forward, "for greatness. His ambition outweighed his talent, but the young artist set out on his date ... with *destiny*."

I laughed again and felt my cheeks flush. "I feel like an ass for not going on that job interview."

She shrugged. "The money was crap anyway. Who cares?"

"It was," I agreed. "And if this all goes to shit, I intend to blame your encouragement."

"That's fine, so long as I get all the credit for the success."

"Deal. Somehow I think you'll keep my feet on the earth."

She lifted her bare feet and stuck them between my legs. "Where else would they be, unless they were in someone's lap?" My hands found them and I looked out the window again, at the façade of the building across the street, lights beginning to come on to silhouette the occupants within. A moment later she had straddled me and her tongue was in my ear, and I laid her back on the loveseat and set about removing her clothing and then mine.

Fall, 1995

I woke up to warble of an uneven alarm. Carissa slapped it violently before turning sleepily into me, naked and warm and perfect. We held each other, falling back asleep until an identical warble brought us both awake again, this time more irritably. She rolled, smacked the alarm again, and then turned it off. Her side of the bed was against the wall, so she climbed over me ungracefully and stood, naked, stretching and yawning by the door. She wrapped a robe around herself and headed toward the bathroom. I reluctantly got out of bed as well, pulling on boxer shorts and padding over to the kitchen to brew coffee. Amy was ensconced behind her purple curtain. When Carissa reappeared, we drank coffee in the purple twilight, whispering a tiredly functional conversation.

"How was your shower?"

"Wet. What are you doing today?"

"Gotta get clothes for the new job."

"Ah, that's right. Wanna do dinner tonight?"

"Sure. Come to my place?"

A nod.

I walked her to the subway station, kissed her, and turned back toward the East Village. As I approached an alleyway on Avenue A between Thirteenth and Twelfth, I saw a New York City firefighter casually smoking a cigarette and leaning on the building's corner. A dead homeless man lay on his back, eyes wide and unblinking and just beginning to haze. Both of the man's hands were frozen into claws and held next to the face, as if he had been frightened to death. I stopped. It was just after nine on a Monday morning and there was a dead man lying in an alleyway.

"Sidewalk's for walkin'," a tattooed and leather-clad man mumbled as he passed, bumping my right shoulder.

The fireman looked at me. "Why don't you shove off, pal." His voice was like a parody of a New York City accent.

I shoved off back to my apartment, changed, and ate some cereal while thinking about the dead man, chewing thoughtfully on store brand Rice Krispies, something called "Krispy Rice." I ate standing because I didn't have any tables or chairs yet, just a lumpy pullout couch I didn't feel like sitting on.

I hadn't gone to the interview in publishing but had found a job in catering, up at the New York Academy of Medicine. It paid seventeen dollars an hour, a near-fortune for me and twice what the full time job would have paid. The math was writer-simple: I could work half as much and make the same amount. That meant more time for writing, more time for living, more time to see the glorious ruin that was the East Village.

I needed catering clothes. My new boss, a caustic balding man with a habit of playing with his balls and commenting on the odor there, told me the cheapest place to buy clothes was SOHO.

"Some fuckin' towelhead runs it," he had said, leaving me at a loss about what ethnicity that insult was aimed toward. I imagined a regal Sikh with piercing black eyes and matching beard. "But he gets cheap shit."

I walked across town to the address I'd been given, crossing Broadway and slipping through the stopped traffic at a red light. I was passing behind a white delivery van as it honked at the cab in front of it. The cab stopped.

"Come on, asshole," the van's driver shouted out the window, startling me. "Get going or go back to where you came from!"

The cab door flew open and a stocky man with dark hair matted down each loaf-like arm got out with his fists clenched. From the curb I looked back.

"Go back ta where I come from," the cabbie bellowed. "Where's dat, you fuckin' asshole? *Brooklyn?*" He cocked a fat fist and smashed it into the other man's face, three times, before the van screeched away. "Fuck you," the cabbie yelled, shaking his fist in the air before getting into his cab and mashing the gas.

I stepped into a store that looked like it sold thrift: threadbare carpet, harsh lighting from a stained drop ceiling, and rows of clothing stacked so densely together the stock could easily have filled a store twice its size.

A man who looked to be Indian or Pakistani, with an impossibly thick head of hair avalanched to one side, glanced up. He wore an ill-fitting white shirt that clung too tightly to his chest, showing off a belly shaped like a basketball. Cheap gold necklaces and rings hung as heavy on his neck and fingers as his equally cheap cologne on his body.

"Yes yes, hello. You are looking to buying clothing today?" he asked.

"My boss told me — "

"Yes yes. What kind of job you working for?"

"Catering."

"Yes yes. Catering work is good work. Good money you make with the catering. Here, in back. You get two shirts in case you spilling on one, yes? I give you special prices. Special prices on two."

"Okay," I said.

He led me toward the middle of the store, glancing at my body before pulling shirts out and handing them to me.

"And you take these pants because you need not ironing them. Tough. Give you special prices on them, too. You buy two I give you second pair fifty percent off."

"I'm new to the city," I ventured. "Only been here a few weeks."

Ignoring my statement, he picked out a clip-on bow tie and a black vest. "Special price today on all these." He flashed very white teeth. "You saving lots of monies."

"Okay. Thanks."

"Yes yes. You just be sure to telling people you working with. Clothes are good, and they are cheap. Strong and well made. I know where come from — yes yes — my uncle owning the factory so special deal and wheel I get. Give special deal and wheel for your friends too."

"Right."

"Would you liking some special clothing for a night out with lady friend? We have lots of specials deals today!"

"No thank you."

Undeterred, he pulled out a yellow polyester shirt and held it up. "Seventy-five percent off!"

I shook my head and he deftly slipped it back. He tallied up the prices and applied the various discounts, showing me how much I saved on each item.

"You see?"

"Yeah man, I got it," I said, growing irritated, which prompted him show me those big white teeth again. He put my clothes into a thin plastic bag.

"You telling your friends," he said, nodding this head.

I took the bag and left without another word. Walking across the city, I noticed that the intensity of the traffic and the people seemed more subdued, more like simple background noise instead of a constant assault on my senses. I was, I realized, starting to feel at home in New York City.

Tuesday

This shows the sales cycle as it currently exists," Steve says, glancing around the long table in Rectangle. His beard looks especially perfect today, and his green shirt and jeans as crisp and fresh as if they'd been pressed just a few moments before. I marvel at his ability to keep them from wrinkling, even in the post-6:00 meetings where my entire body feels crumpled and my clothes look like they were pulled from the bottom of a hamper.

Jamie is directly across from Steve and me, ensconced in a blue blazer and white collared shirt. Jen sits next to her, blonde hair pulled into a ponytail, blue eyes rimmed in red. She has a six-month-old at home, and I suspect that some days she comes to work on a few hours sleep, if any. That doesn't dent her frightening level of professionalism and work output. What all four of us share is a willingness to take part in the gamble of the startup world.

Tech startups work under a simple premise: employees get equity. If the company goes public or gets bought out, that equity turns into cash. People at startups tend to work harder and at higher risk of losing their jobs than in more conventional companies, but their risk is offset by a chance to strike it rich.

Equity is like the splitting of a pie. When a company starts, the pie is tiny and a few people have really big pieces of it. Because the company isn't worth anything yet, their large percentages of shares are also essentially worthless. They have big slices of a tiny pie. Executives and investors get the biggest slices, as well as what are called preferred stocks. In the event of a buyout or sale, preferred stocks get paid first and at many times the rate of common stock. This matters because a company can sell itself and make the board, venture capitalists, and executives very rich, while leaving the rank and file better off than they were, but far from wealthy.

Some of this stock — both common and preferred — is set aside as an option pool for future employees. Companies go through rounds of funding — A round, B round, and so forth. Startups are, by definition, usually running at a loss and need the funding rounds to continue doing things like paying the salaries of their employees, making products, and keeping the lights on. Once they spend the money from a round, they need to point to growth and stability and then ask for more money to operate in the next round. If the company misses a funding round, it will usually go bankrupt in a matter of weeks or months.

The reason this matters is that Jen's red eyes, Steve' meteoric rise into the executive level at the expense of his waistline, Jamie's cutting intelligence, and my willingness to take my first full time job are all based on us working with this calculated risk: bust your ass for a company in a startup phase, and you might — *might* — end up with a few million in your bank account if the company goes public or gets bought by a bigger fish. A big *if* and a big *or*, but the potential is there to make a lot of money in a way that a conventional company can't touch. Put less kindly, the four of us are united more by greed than by any kind of idealism or loyalty to a company.

Trudent, the company I work for, is in the almost unimaginably dull field of corporate compliance: the forgotten, adopted stepchild of a corporation's family. To use the Titanic metaphor, most compliance departments spring into action the moment their ship hits an iceberg — an employee breaking the law, a manager sexually harassing a subordinate, a conspiracy to defraud, or a hundred other potentially fatal places a company can get sunk by the behavior of its workers. Trudent is trying to change that and help corporations avoid the icebergs altogether, through technology, and make a ton of money in the process.

Trudent, being a tech company, has built software to automate how compliance operates. The promise is that the software can analyze huge data pools inside big companies and actually identify hot spots before major problems emerge. Steve, and the entire executive staff for that matter, didn't know a damn thing about corporate compliance before they started. But as technologists, they did know how to upend an industry twenty years behind the times.

Behind Jen and Jamie is a large monitor, and on it a PowerPoint Steve is referring to as he talks. "You can see we were looking to sell $900K in net new ACV, with $100K in new customers expansion? The pipeline for Q1 is $6.4 million, and we're looking like we're going to meet that goal, which is more than I expected this month. Michael will love this." Michael is the CEO. He's not much older than me, which is both inspiring and insulting.

"We all know," Steve continues, "that Michael's a passionate man, likes to get things done right. These numbers are going to make him a little more fun to be around."

Michael has been away on numerous business trips and I've only met him in passing during my three months there.

"So he's not normally fun to be around?" I ask, with a self-effacing smile designed to hide the seriousness of the question.

Jen glances up with eyes looking as if they might leak tears of blood. "When we go to trade shows, he's been known to be — " she pauses. "An *intense* presence." She exchanges a glance with Jamie.

"He likes to get things right," Steve says by way of apology, "because they matter. The details matter. *All* the details. He's out getting the funding, after all, and he's the face of the company, and we're getting close to our C round. In fact, it's looking like we're going to get another board member, which is going to help us secure more funding? All the numbers have to be right, as you all know, and we have to make sure we're doing our part to bring leads into the sales team."

"We've learned," Jen says with a smile that looks wilted at the edges, "to keep Michael away from trade shows until we're set up and ready for him."

"It only happened *once* this year," Steve notes, "so we're ahead of last year."

I'm intrigued. "I'm sensing a story."

Steve taps his hands on the table quickly. "Let's not get into TMI here," he quips, looking back to the PowerPoint.

"Oh, let's throw Logan a bone," says Jamie, eyes rolling. "He's a big boy and it's good to know." She continues without waiting for approval. "It was Chicago. Our biggest trade show. We made the mistake of letting Michael into the building before we were ready, and he didn't react well to what he saw. Of course we weren't set up yet and things were really a mess with only about an hour until things kicked off, but he really flipped his wig. I didn't envy that phone call he made to you, Steve. At least you took the bullet for us. I only got grazed." She pursed her lips in a kind of half smile.

Steve makes a dismissive gesture with his right hand. "Comes with the territory." He glances at Jamie. "Plus I think he's a little intimidated by you. But yeah, I told him everything was taken care of. And it was. It was all fine." He pauses. "But yeah. We don't let him near the booth now."

It sounds to me that *passionate* might be code for *asshole*.

"So," Steve continues, "back to this work of art," he indicates the PowerPoint, "and our focus on customer expansion this quarter. I should note," he says, lightly and with a touch of self-mockery, "that I did this PowerPoint myself. Not too bad, if I do say so." The PowerPoint is, in fact, quite well designed. "Maybe I should be the new designer."

"You're a regular Renaissance man," I say.

"Hardly," he laughs. Jamie's head is bent over her computer. Her black-rimmed glasses reflect the white light off her screen, and at the moment Steve is about to move on to the next slide, she speaks up. "You misspelled 'expansion.'"

I look up to the huge monitor facing us. Sure enough, *Customer Expamsion* is clearly worded there. Jamie's expression all business while Steve's is slack. Bright red patches rise to his cheeks and forehead. Jen's hand goes to the front of her face, laughter corralled behind her fingers.

"I wasn't *really* bragging about the design," he says, offering a chirp of a laugh. "I *know* I'm no designer."

"Sorry to interrupt," Jamie deadpans, tossing her hair off her left shoulder. "You were saying something about customer expamsion?"

Fall, 1995

Underneath the East Village's artistic and beatnik façade were layers of hell, a Dante's inferno of New Yorkers. All over Tomkins Square Park were the junkies, part of the lowest level. They'd given up fighting their collapse and instead embraced it in a way that bordered on bravery. They got as high as their wasted bodies allowed, shuffling behind their shopping carts, gathering in dark corners where they could shun the daylight, shooting up between parked cars and spread fingers, and looking at anyone not like them with hollowed and suspicious eyes. Yet among themselves addiction had obliterated any relevance of race or gender or age.

Above the junkies were the men and women in dark clothes with bruised circles under their eyes who emerged in the later afternoons and gained energy as the night deepened. Pale and thin and no longer fully of our world, they moved as if trying to shake off a nightmare. I'd see them in the pizza parlors and corner diners, talking to each other in hushed tones, arms carefully covered by leather even when the late afternoon sun made the city uncomfortably warm.

And then there were those who had fallen through the cracks of the city, those trying to make a buck to get them through today and, if they were lucky, tomorrow. They were the stranded young men and women of the projects, too under-educated and too abandoned by the city's services to escape the gravity well of poverty. They were the failed middle-aged white artists circling the drain of their dreams, too stubborn to start over and too old to break through. They were the foreign-born owners of the bodegas and Chinese restaurants making just enough to live five deep in one-room apartments, imprisoned by the hope of the American dream.

Interspersed between these strata were others. Some like me: drawn to the Village for its cheap rent, using it for inspiration, entertainment, and, most of all, access. The East Village consisted of worlds tucked inside worlds like so many Russian nesting dolls, all bound together inside five tight square blocks.

On an early October afternoon I left my apartment to meet my brother at Nino's Pizza, on St. Mark's and Avenue A. It sat across the street from one of my favorite bars, Alcatraz, an open-walled dive that served cheap pitchers of stale beer on weeknights. Franklin, taller than most, appeared over the crowd half a block up St. Mark's, moving with great efficiency through the slower, shorter bodies.

His hair was cropped close on the sides and back, with graying temples even though he was still comfortably in his twenties. He wore round sunglasses, jeans, and a black fitted T-shirt tucked into his pants, with a thick leather belt that had pronounced white stitching. His portfolio, a large black case, hung heavily at his side.

"Let's eat," he said, forgoing a greeting. "I'm starving."

"Sure. How was it? The gallery?"

We got in line for the outside counter at Nino's. Franklin took off his sunglasses and slipped them into the collar of his shirt. "The woman who owns it is nice. British. Think it's her husband's money behind the gallery. We hit it off. She really liked my work. She's going to get back to me about a possible solo show."

I smiled at my brother. I knew him well enough to read between the lines. "British woman, rich husband, owns gallery, likes young handsome artist. Am I getting the subtext correct?"

He started to say something, then thought twice about it, and offered his own smile instead. "If talent alone were enough, Logan, I'd already be famous."

I laughed and he smiled and, as was often the case with his comments, I couldn't tell where sarcasm ended and truth began.

"You haven't met Alejandro, right?" he asked, changing the subject.

I shook my head. "Nope. You guys teach together?"

"Uh-huh. He might join us here if he's done with his appointment in time. Told him we'd be here at noon." He checked his watch. "Gimme a Sicilian," Franklin said to the scruffy man behind the counter, who nodded and looked to me.

"Regular slice," I said. "Extra crispy."

"They all extra crispy, my friend. This is New York. Drink?"

"Two Cokes."

"Eight bucks, my friend."

Franklin handed over ten. "I got it. Keep the change."

"Thank you, my friend."

Our slices came up a few moments later, and we took them across the street to a park bench.

"School okay?"

Franklin nodded. He taught at Pratt in Brooklyn. "Paycheck and healthcare. Is there another reason to teach?"

"Those impressionable young minds?"

"Fuck 'em. Ah, there's Alejandro." Franklin waved an arm.

A short man with his head held high and chest pushed forward was coming toward us. He wore black jeans, skin tight, and a white top that narrowed at the waist but was flowing at the shoulder. It was open to his mid-chest. Alejandro's hair looked like a push broom turned on end, a mass of jet black bristles standing on his head as though glued there. Large, boxy sunglasses hid a small face. Despite his small stature, his swagger took the space of a bodybuilder.

"Hey," he said, taking a seat next to Franklin. He put the back of his hand on his forehead and wiped away a line of sweat. "Fuck *me*," he announced. "Baby is *hot*."

"That's because it's hot today," Franklin stated. "You wanna slice? We'll slow down."

"Honey," Alejandro said, "this body doesn't watch *itself*. If I eat pizza now I'll have to purge later. Or worse: go to the gym." He looked around. "But I will do a beer."

I laughed, thinking he was joking.

"Too early, you fucking lush. This is Logan, my brother."

"The writer?"

"That's the one."

I felt my cheeks flush at being called *the writer*. Alejandro pulled his sunglasses down to reveal brown eyes and groomed eyebrows and extended his hand across Franklin like he was the belle of the ball. I took it.

"Handsome," he said, glancing at Franklin. "You're all pasty, Franklin — he's all dark. How did that happen?"

"Mystery of genetics," Franklin said, tearing off a slice of pizza. "So how'd it go?"

Alejandro sighed and sat back, pushing his sunglasses back up. "Bitches. They don't know art when they see it, I'm telling you. I thought they'd like this photography — it's right up their alleyway. I spent a month in the fucking projects of Harlem risking my life shooting that shit. But I didn't get a good feeling."

"Maybe all that empathy came through," Franklin said.

"I'm gay. I can't discriminate. I can only discern."

Franklin snorted a little through his nose. "The vodka stank on you probably didn't help."

Alejandro looked horrified. "I showered, lotioned, *and* cologned this morning. I do *not* smell of last night."

"Those aren't even verbs."

"One of them was. Besides, *cunting* isn't a word. As in, stop cunting me."

I gave a laugh. Franklin just shook his head. "We had a few drinks last night, but I left and went home at two." He turned back to Alejandro. "What time did *you* leave?"

"Oh, honey," he sighed. "It was an ugly morning."

Franklin smirked at him. "How ugly?"

Alejandro sat back, exhaling deeply and looking straight ahead. "I felt like Marilyn Monroe the next day." He swallowed, and then looked over the tops of his sunglasses at us. "*If* she'd lived."

Fall, 1995

It was ten when we finally left the apartment. Carissa and I walked the twenty-five blocks from her place to the West Village. The summer's heat had dissipated into the lengthening nights of a new season and the city had a subdued, calm feel to it. The jazz bar I'd read about was tucked off an alleyway and we almost missed its sign. We went up a narrow flight of stairs and through a single door into a small, rectangular club that seated maybe a hundred people. It was already half full and smoky but we were able to snag a table, a major coup in New York City on a Friday night. As I got a round of drinks, Carissa started talking to a woman at the table next to ours.

"Logan," Carissa said as I sat back down. Her green eyes were bright. "This is Anna. She's also an aspiring writer."

I winced a little at that adjective. "Nice to meet you," I said.

"You too," Anna said sweetly. "Always nice to meet another crazy person. Carissa was just telling me that you guys have only been in the city for a few months."

I nodded.

"How's it treating you?"

"You know, I'm not really sure how to answer that question."

She nodded. "New York can be a bit much at first. You know what Anaïs Nin said?"

"No."

"Who's Anaïs Nin?" Carissa asked.

"She's one of the first writers of female erotica, from the mid twentieth century."

"And then some," I added.

Anna nodded. "She said something like, 'New York is the opposite of Paris. People aren't concerned with intimacy. No attention is given to friendship,

33

and nothing is done to soften the harshness of life.' I love that. So honest. So true." Anna looked at the two of us. "It's hard to stay open to strangers here."

I nodded again. Anna took a sip of beer. She seemed a few years older than Carissa and me, with dark hair that ended abruptly in bangs and large brown eyes. She had the kind of face that at first seemed plain, but the more you looked at it the more attractive it became. Her skin was dark and smooth, and her elongated neck was wrapped in a fashionable red scarf. A black sweater was tight enough to outline a shapely figure, and black boots were pulled halfway to the knee over her jeans.

"What do you write?" Anna asked me. The bar was filling up, and we had to speak loudly to hear each other.

"Fiction." Then feeling instantly uncomfortable, I threw a question on top of it. "What about you?"

"What kind of fiction?"

Fuck. "Literary, I suppose."

"Influences?"

"Oh, you know. The usual suspects. DeDillo. Joyce. Pynchon. Agee. Hemingway, of course. Burgess."

"No women," she said with a smile. "Interesting."

"I like female writers too," I countered. "How can you not love O'Conner? I've also read Rand. Atwood. Wolfe. Butler. Lee. Cather. Austen — "

"Okay *okay*," she said, putting up her hands and laughing. "You're off the hook!"

"A good writer is a good writer," I pressed. "Gender's not very important to me."

"I wish I had the that luxury."

I raised my eyebrows but she changed the subject. "The writers in your first list — the men — were all postmodern. Or mostly. Is that the kind of writing you do?"

"Not so much. More modernist." The truth was I'd started a novel, but it was also true that I was completely lost in it. I had no idea if it was modern or postmodern, and didn't really care at that point.

"You?"

"Mine is literary fiction, and strongly postmodern," she said, quickly and confidently. "I got my first story published last year in the *Antioch Review*."

"Woah." The *Antioch Review* was an established and serious literary magazine, and one that had rejected not one but two of my stories. My jaw reflexively clenched.

"And now?"

"Oh, I'm drowning in a novel," she sighed, brown eyes glancing up toward the darkened ceiling. She tapped her hands on the table. "Short stories are a lot easier."

Carissa looked expectantly at me as if waiting for me to collude.

"There's no money in short stories," I noted.

"But you love writing them," Carissa offered hopefully.

"That's true."

Anna smiled and leaned closer, putting a hand on my forearm, "I'm thinking of applying to Iowa next year, you know, to build more connections and maybe make some money teaching."

"University of Iowa. The famous alma mater of Flannery O'Conner and Tennessee Williams. Tough to get into," I observed.

She shrugged. "I have an undergrad degree from Columbia. Did pretty well there; made some contacts."

"Oh."

"You?"

"I'm more a state college kind of guy. My most of my contacts are still busy drinking beer in their sixth year of school. I probably should have said that it would be tough for *me* to get into Iowa."

She laughed.

"So you're hedging your bets with a degree. That's great, *if* you want to teach. But you have to be careful it doesn't take the fight out of you."

Anna laughed, a good-natured chuckle that expanded to show her white teeth. "Fight? Goodness, I don't know if I think of my writing as a *fight*."

I sat back and looked at her with what I imagined was an expression of genuine surprise. This might have been one of those moments when someone holds up a mirror and in the reflection you see yourself with such clarity it changes the course of your life. Yet I considered what Anna had said with my clenching jaw and hand firmly wrapped around my pint and dismissed it entirely and immediately.

Anna turned to Carissa. The two of them started to talk, smiling and laughing often.

As I looked through the smoke of the bar to the stage, it took a moment for me to exhale fully and drop my shoulders away from my ears. I rolled my head around my neck and sat back.

The stage was not much bigger than a four-person dinner table and, as I was wat"ching it, a heavy-set woman took a seat behind a tiny drum set consisting of only a snare and a single cymbal. She was so large her bulk hung over the seat in every direction. Two rail-thin men, one with a cigarette hanging out of his mouth, stepped out of the crowd and stood on either side of her, all three dark of skin and dressed as if headed to a New Orleans Christmas ball. The men wore dark suits with white ties and fedoras; the woman a black dress with a white scarf tied around her neck. If there had been a fourth person, he would have needed to stand off the stage.

"Well well," the woman said into the mic. Her voice was as big and full as a summer thunderstorm, and it rolled through the club. "Here we be," she rumbled, rattling the snare, "at Mondo Cane in the West

Village on a Friday night, in New York City. Mmm mm." A few people whooped and clapped hands. "Y'all ready to hear some *bluuues*?" She stretched out the last word.

The room cheered.

"Well, shiiiiit. All right then. Y'all are in for a treat. We're the Bass Tones; I'm Loretta, with Tyco B on base and Little Jimmy on the ghee-tar. This first one's an old, old Tommy Johnson ditty from back in the Dust Bowl days, a little something we could all use t'night, a little *Canned Heat Blues*." The band crept into the song.

The show ended a few hours later. Anna and her friends said their goodbyes and headed for the stairs that went down to the street. One too many beers forced Carissa and me to wait in the insanely long line for the single bathroom in the bar.

Once relieved, we began the long walk back toward her apartment. It was mild and clear, and a few stars poked through the streetlights over our heads.

"Can you do me a favor," I asked, having to speak carefully around my own tongue.

"Sure, baby."

"Can you not call me an *aspiring* writer?"

Carissa looked up at me, almost startled. "But you're not published!"

"I know. I *know* I am an aspiring writer," I said, laughing and shaking my head. "But I still don't want to be *called* one. Look, I've written almost half a dozen short stories and I've started a novel. I think I've passed the *aspiring* part and am *actually* a writer, even if I haven't gotten published yet. It's stupid. Semantics and all of that. But it's ... "

"Sure, baby," she said, easily, "that's fine with me. I didn't mean to insult you."

"I wasn't insulted," I said, now feeling foolish. "You don't have to apologize. I'm fine, really, it's just, it's a lotta work, you know? The

37

sacrifice and all that. *Aspiring* makes me feel like I'm some housewife dabbling in arts and crafts."

Carissa laughed. "You'd make a lousy housewife."

"And how."

In overalls and a giant pea coat, she looked as if her clothes were swallowing her. Only her little face peeked out from the layers, scarves, and hat. Third Avenue was strangely quiet for a Friday night. We passed a pub, a kind common in those days, which had managed to survive the eighties without making a single interior design modification.

"Look at this place!" I said, stopping. "The half-burned-out Christmas lights!"

"An aqua bar," Carissa gasped, looking in through the door. "That's pure, exotic *plastic*!"

"A Schlitz neon sign! *Schlitz*! Do they even still make that?"

She pulled the scarf away from her face. "Oh my God — brown carpet on the front of the bar. Facing the barstools."

"And those barstools! That's brown vinyl, one hundred percent. Oh baby, we *have* to."

She nodded. "Yes. Yes we do."

A balding man halfway down the bar glanced up as we came in. He wore a white T-shirt stained with beer and had two or three days of graying stubble across a weak-chinned face. His tan, such as it was, ended a few inches short of his shirtsleeves, exposing pale skin between the elbow and cuff. Carissa and I sat down in the brown high-back chairs that were spilling their stuffing through fissures. There were a dozen people in the bar, mostly older and working class. "What'll ya have?" he asked in a thick Irish accent.

"A Guinness," I said. "Gin and tonic for the lady."

"Need age cards," he said. "Ya look like ya only seen a few donkey years."

We exchanged a look.

"Donkey years?" Carissa asked.

"Y'er too young to even know the expression, darlin'."

"Uh, okay?"

We showed him our IDs.

"Own shoes older than the lot of you," he said to her. He turned to me and looked at my date of birth. "And socks older than you."

"It might be time to do some shopping," Carissa noted. He raised an eyebrow at her but didn't smile. I laughed.

"The Gat'll take awhile, mate, just so ya know. We pour 'em proper."

"Righteous," I said to a look that wasn't sure if I had offered genuine appreciation or New York sarcasm.

The gin and tonic came quickly and, true to the bartender's word, the Guinness took another five minutes. But when it did arrive it was poster-perfect. An Imperial pint, twenty ounces instead of the American sixteen, settled fully with just a millimeter of white, foamed head on the top.

"That's gorgeous," I said, but the bartender ignored me, probably having decided I was, in fact, an asshole.

"Anna — the aspiring writer — was talking about getting an MFA," Carissa said, with a smirk. "Okay if I call other aspiring writers aspiring?"

"Oh, it's gonna be like that, is it?"

"Well," she said, "I just want to watch out for sensitive artists' feelings."

"Oh ha ha," I said.

She laughed and her green eyes caught the lights behind the bar, flashing at me. "Her plan for an MFA seemed like a smart idea."

I shook my head. "If you wanna part with $80K. A master's to learn how to write? You don't become an artist in school, you become one the streets," I declared. "MFAs are for teachers, not artists."

Carissa put her hand on my arm. "Logan, darling, that is either the truest or the most pretentious thing you've ever said."

My drink caught in my throat, and I dislodged it with laughter. "A little too binary, perhaps?"

"We'll just have to wait to see which it is. Could be a genius statement. Still," she said, "I bet you would be able to network like crazy in a school like Iowa."

"Sure," I said. "But they'd never let a guy like me in. That's Ivy League, and that isn't me."

"But you have your stories. They're good."

"Yeah, but I haven't been published anywhere. I'm just another hack out here who thinks he's a writer."

"An *aspiring* one," Carissa corrected.

"Oh," I said, narrowing my eyes at her, "you're really asking for it!" I paused. "Truthfully, yeah, exactly that. I just don't like it when *you* say it. Besides, we live in New York City, baby. I can network like crazy *here*. Franklin's connected. An MFA. Fuck. It's only good for a tenured existence far removed from the front lines of life."

Carissa looked at me, and the playfulness left us as her smile waned. She spoke quietly. "I don't know if I want to live on the front lines of life, Logan. Life isn't a fight."

My stomach twisted at the comment. I was clinging to my newfound identity like a lost man to his compass. Carissa had just tried to snatch it out of my hands.

"What do you know about fights?" I countered, my words crisp with anger. "You couldn't even finish your freshman year of school." I'd fought my way through grade school, with students and teachers alike; fought the system and my parents in high school and been arrested multiple times in my defiance; fought to get a scholarship so I could afford to go to university and then fought the professors I didn't like while there. In New York City at twenty-one years of age, everything everywhere seemed a fight.

Looking down the bar, Carissa didn't respond. Her green eyes narrowed and I felt my heart beating somewhere in my stomach. I was ready for this fight. *Bring it on*, I thought.

"I didn't want to give back my freshman fifteen," she said at last.

I opened my mouth, but realized after a long moment that I didn't understand what she meant. "*What?*"

"My freshman fifteen. I didn't want to give it back."

I blinked. It was a joke. A joke. And a good one. Reluctantly, I allowed myself to smile, then chuckle.

"I hate to tell you," I said, "but I think you're back down to your fighting weight."

"Thanks, baby. But I'll find those lost pounds. Don't you worry." She looked ahead with mock intensity, like she was stepping into a ring. "They're *mine*."

I laughed, and she turned and gave me one of her open smiles, like I could see all the way to her heart. "And yes. I hated school. No shame in that."

"Nope." My anger was gone with my next exhale. "I know you hated it, and you did the smart thing, which was stop wasting money on something you don't like and get busy living instead." I took a sip of my Guinness. Carissa's hand found mine and I squeezed it. We sat in silence as the bartender walked past, looking dutifully at the level of our drinks before moving on without saying a word.

"This one is mine to lose," I almost whispered. "It might not be easy, and it might take me to my knees once or twice, but I know I've got what it takes."

"Just don't go fifteen rounds only to lose by decision, Rocky."

I felt a sting and tried to pull my hand away, but she grasped it. "Hang on," she said. "Hang on. Boy, you're really wound tight around this. I'm sorry, baby. I know how important it is to you. If you're gonna step into that ring, I've got your back. One hundred percent." She swiveled her chair to me. "I know you, Logan. I know it's better for you to fight and lose than spend the rest of your life wondering what it might have been like. I know that much about you." She smiled a little, mostly to herself, looking down at her white and pink sneakers. "I love that about you. That you're willing to lose rather than not to try at all. Not that I *think* you'll lose." She thought a moment and then shook her head. "What I'm trying to say is just maybe it's not a fight you're heading into. Like Anna said."

I'd already forgotten what Anna said but it came back to me with all the sting of ignored truth. I nodded but didn't fully let her warning in. It, and the conversation, would all come back eighteen months later when my world went dark and everything in it was taken from me.

She took my other hand. "No matter what, I'm here for you, Logan. All the way."

I fought back a hitch of emotion that threatened to embarrass me with tears or, worse, a sob, and turned her hands over in mine, those little hands with their little fingers and little fingernails painted green and flaking off to show the clear nails underneath. I took a breath to steady myself. "I'm fucking crazy about you," I said at last, my voice controlled. "I couldn't do this without you. I couldn't do *anything* without you. I wouldn't want to."

"I know," she said, smiling in the shy way she did when I complimented her directly, and wiping her eyes with the back of her hand, looking very young. "I know, baby."

Tuesday Night

I'm sitting at our kitchen table. It's a gorgeous piece of furniture, actually. A rectangular slab long enough to seat eight comfortably, made of blonde and dense wood a friend told me looked like a tree native to South Africa. Whatever its origin, it's a nice place to think and work. And eat.

Our townhouse is one grand room downstairs with the kitchen at the rear. It's an end unit, so one of our walls is filled with windows, their tan curtains now drawn against the night. Two lights hang low above the table, shining directly into the surface like miniature beams of sunlight. I'm sitting at the end closest to our front door.

"It's the first piece, one of five," she says, looking up and across the stove at me. She's wearing white pajamas, heavy cotton for the cool fall weather, and a red robe. Her hair is down and full around her face, looking almost black in the low light. She's magnificent, regal, and her beauty never fails to penetrate to my core, although these days she feels more a piece of art that touches from behind a frame and across a distance of a few feet. "Can you just read over it, see if it can be any better?"

I take a sip of wine, a nice Bordeaux I picked up on sale. It feels velvety and soft as it swirls around my mouth. "Of course. Just share it in Google docs. What's the idea?"

"I'm trying to create a story to build trust. Then make the offer in a way that triggers scarcity, which I have to handle very carefully so that people sign up for my training. It has to be subtle. I want you to tell me if you think it's working or if it's too heavy-handed."

"Why not just make the offer? You're selling coaching, after all, not sneakers."

She shakes her head. "We talked about this. You know I tried that. The last two trainings. I didn't use any of the marketing tricks, and both fell pretty much flat. Or at least didn't get the kinds of numbers I was wanting." She is very precise in how she speaks. Each word is crafted like it's been carefully curated before being allowed to emerge, whole, and as part of the larger exhibition.

I nod. "Right. I remember."

"People say they don't want that, but then they don't put their money where their mouths are." She shakes her head.

"So what's your story?"

"That's the challenge. It's basically life coaching, but there are a lot of us out there now. What's the thing that makes me stand out from the crowd and not just be another coach?"

"That's a good question." I tap my left hand on the dense wood. "That's the million-dollar marketing question, in fact. What did you come up with?"

"Well, my embodiment. The story about how a yoga practice kept me grounded through the death of my grandfather; that part of what I can teach, aside from business and money and that kind of stuff, is also the more esoteric, things like yoga and meditation."

"Not bad." I consider. "But I'm curious: do you have to always have to talk about yourself and your life in your marketing?"

"My life *is* my work," she snaps. The room seems to cool by a degree or two. She lifts the mug of tea in front of her heart, with both hands, and I see her next sentence being constructed. "It's what makes me different from other coaches out there."

I nod again, warily. "Okay. Okay." She doesn't make a demarcation between her vocation and herself, which means there's really no off switch. Many — these days it feels like most — of our conversations involve her work, even though I know I should be sharing more of my own struggles. "Okay," I repeat.

"You don't like my idea?"

I consider my words carefully. "Well, what are you doing that's different from 'just coaching'?"

"You know what. I just told you."

"Tell me in a line or two."

She thinks, and the cup comes back down to rest on the stove. "Finding your ground — especially when the world is pulling the rug out from under your feet."

"Nice. Okay. That's not really what you said before, which is why I asked. Do you have a story you can tell where you learned that?"

"How the body — having an embodiment practice — kept me grounded in one of the most ungrounded times in my life."

"That's a lot closer to what your special sauce is, right? That thing that makes you unique?"

She sighs and then smiles tiredly. "I guess. I kind of hate this."

I smile. "Yeah, marketing kind of sucks. But it's this or get a real job."

She shakes her head and smiles at me for the first time. "Not that!"

I laugh. "No, not that."

"Okay, I'll see where I can take it."

"You still need me to read the copy?"

"Just read the first one. The rest I'll rewrite."

"Okay."

She moves out from the kitchen, sitting at the head of the table and looking at me. Her eyes are brown and clear and sober.

"Are you okay?" she asks.

I'm taken aback. "What?"

"You just look tired. Your eyes." She bites the inside of her lip and looks down.

"I'm having some trouble sleeping," I admit. "Not feeling all that great, to be honest."

She puts her hand, warmed from the hot cup of tea, on mine. "I know you're having a tough time with the job and all," she says. "I'm sorry."

"Thank you." I hesitate. "I've wondered if I should just quit," I say, both to her and to myself. We sit in silence. She is good at times like these, giving me space to discover where my thoughts are looking to take me. "I hate it there." The admission is surprising to me, and I do the thing I'm so good at doing, which is to push down the darkness that tries to rise up and out of me. I clear my throat and drink more wine.

She nods. "I know it's hard. And we talked about this: it's a good investment because of the stock. Worth another eight or nine months."

"I know," I say. "I guess I just didn't expect to feel this stuck. This unhappy."

She looks into her tea for a moment, the right corner of her mouth pulling upwards the way it does when she's struggling with an idea.

"Have you thought about getting a different job?"

I exhale. "Sure, but it's not the job itself." Again I have to slow down and find my way through my own thoughts, since that sentence is, strangely, news to me. "Everybody there is fine, as far as jobs go. A different job would just be … another job. Like the same station but a different tune." I look down into my wine. Sediment is settling to the bottom of the glass. I make a mental note to not finish it. "I've managed to avoid real jobs for most of my forty-odd years on this planet. Catering. Bartending. Freelancing. Anything to not have to sit under a row of lights, and … " I shrug. There's something dark and sinewy trying to come up through my belly and into my throat, like vomit. I swallow.

She's been watching my downturned face. The warm hand squeezes. "I'm proud of you," she says. "I know it's not easy." I look up into her eyes, shocked when a hard sob rolls through my body. Instinctually I cover my face with my left hand and withdraw my right from hers. Two more sobs rise through me before I'm able to gain control again. I exhale.

"Phew," I say, "sorry about that. I'm just tired, is all."

Her eyes want to comfort me, yet they seem impossibly far away. I realize that I don't know what it is I need, and she doesn't know what to offer, and so her hands end up around her teacup and her eyes cast into it.

"I'm sorry, Logan," she offers. "I know it's hard."

"Maybe I should just quit." This is an empty threat; we both know I can't afford to lose the job.

She goes still. "You could, but try to keep in mind how hard things were before you took that job. The debt. The running out of cash. The fear. The failed book." Her eyes look back to me, and they're not hard. "This isn't perfect, but it can get you back on your feet again. Get you back to a place where you can choose what might be next for you, that isn't in a place you hate."

I stare at that gritty sentiment at the bottom of my glass, and then turn it up and into my mouth. It has the consistency of sand, sticking to my teeth. "I don't hate Trudent. I'm grateful for the paychecks. It's just." I stop there.

"I know," she says, "I understand the nuance."

Of course she does. She's a coach, yes, but she has a Master's and is a capable businesswoman, someone who has built a solid income for herself by not working in an office like I've had to do. Her dreams, of becoming a famous author and teacher, are still nascent. Mine were realized and lost in another era and never recaptured. The book after my first one was stillborn, coming into the world with no life inside of it.

She looks at the clock. "I need to get into bed before it gets any later. Tomorrow ... "

"I know," I say, "I know." I look around the quiet, dark house and spot the whisky sitting on the counter.

"Can you tuck me in?"

"Of course." I put her to bed and go back downstairs to pour the brown liquid into a proper tumbler, dropping in a small piece of ice to release the flavors. It cracks and settles, and I inhale deeply before taking that first, soothing sip. Stepping outside without a coat and in my stocking feet, the cold is intense and the air still. I walk to the curb in front of our townhome and look up into the stars smeared overhead. A million years ago, I'd taken some advanced astronomy classes in college and had been struck that the more I'd learned the more wonder I felt at how tiny and insignificant we really are, how much vaster our ignorance is than our knowledge. The stars burn overhead, many of them long since dead, indifferent to the insignificance of this one, small human gazing upwards with a fleeting sense of wonder.

Late Fall, 1995

The Meat Packing District on the West Side of Manhattan got its name in the most literal fashion. Delivery vans and diesel-spewing, graffiti-covered trucks lined the blocks. Thick-necked men wearing white butcher jackets stained brown from their work hauled slabs of carcasses onto and off of warehouse docks and took cigarette breaks on the sidewalks. Open warehouse doors divulged long stretches of animal cadavers hanging from meat hooks under the glow of hundreds of florescent lights.

The streets themselves were drab cobblestone where warehouses squatted low and wide, accented by faded graffiti and rusting corrugated metal doors. Street-facing windows were heavily barred and grey with filth. Once the sun had set across the Hudson and the workers had gone to their homes in New Jersey and the distant boroughs, it became a staging ground for hookers and dealers.

In the middle of this desert of industry ignored by city zoning enforcers, a few daring clubs had sprouted, using the irony of the neighborhood as a calling card for hipness to the attention-deficit New York night scene.

The five of us walked west through the neighborhood, my brother and I in the lead.

"This part of town really stinks," Amy said, her nose wrinkling.

"Franklin will take us through any foul-smelling shit to get to a party," said Jackson. At twenty-eight, he was the elder statesman of our group.

Blue lights and heavy bass were spilling from the open doors of the industrial space ahead of us, where a long line of men clad in leather or tight-fitting jeans reached along the sidewalk. As we passed catcalls were hurled our way.

"You should change teams! The sex is better and there's no conversation!"

As we passed the open doors, I saw that the party inside was on the scale of a circus. Men in cages hung from the ceiling, shirtless men were everywhere, and there were lights and drinks and cigarettes and shouting. There was a bar visible, bathed in blue lights. Dozens of men stood three-thick at it, a good number of them making out.

"Jesus," I said. "Gay men really know how to party."

Franklin shrugged. "Everybody wants the same thing."

I laughed. "I hadn't thought of it quite that way."

"We close?" Jackson said. "Or did we miss your club back there?"

"Not gay enough for me."

The only two other places within a few blocks were a sadomasochist lounge and sex club and a faux country and western bar. The latter was called Hogs and Heifers, an up-and-coming New York City paradox that would, within a few years, become a cliché: the trendy dive bar. They rather famously didn't have heat and more famously encouraged women to leave their bras hanging behind the bar. The bartenders were always women, always attractive and fit, and always obnoxious. If you dared enter the bar with a tie they would usually cut it off at the knot after stopping the music — and the party — to point out the offender, making a crowd-cheering spectacle of the whole thing.

We pushed through the doors, showed our IDs, and stepped in. Garth Brooks was blaring into a space that was cold, dirty, and badly lit. There was a long bar on the left as we entered, with thousands of bras hanging from every surface and more than a few neckties castrated from their knots. Pool tables were straight ahead and to the right. Bikers, art students, business people, New Jersey cowboys, and bohemian artists were mixing together. Just about everybody was smoking.

We took a collective pause at the door. Jackson hooked his thumbs into his jeans. "No sawdust on the floor? Fuck, they call this country and western?"

"Careful," Franklin warned. "With those white sneakers somebody's liable to hand you a cane and a cup for pennies."

"True; I don't got no three-hundred-dollar cowboy boots to make *me* an authority. What do *you* wrestle? Paintbrushes?"

"Unavailable women. When we need an authority on East Rutherford we know where to look."

"You can look right here," Jackson grabbed his crotch and flashed his teeth. "I'm from fucking Queens."

"And I thought that was a French accent."

"Come on, ladies," Carissa said, smacking Franklin hard on the ass. "Play nice or you won't get any cake. I'll get us a table. Come on, Amy." Amy smiled at Franklin and dragged a finger along his arm as she passed. "Hey, Frenchman," Carissa called, "you're with us. Let the Downing brothers get the first round."

She, Amy, and Jackson walked toward a pool table while Franklin and I headed to the bar.

"Got give it to Amy," I said, "she's discreet." I let the obvious irony of my statement sit a moment. "Might as well hang her bra on your head."

Franklin's face flashed momentary disgust. "You wouldn't believe what I have to endure sometimes."

"Yeah, it's such a burden being tall and handsome and having twenty-one-year-olds throw themselves at you. How do you survive it?"

Franklin smiled tiredly but said nothing.

"Where's Lily?" I asked, referencing Franklin's girlfriend.

"She fancies herself a yogi," Franklin said, scratching the top of his head with his ring finger. "Doesn't drink, doesn't like smoke, doesn't like bars. She would hate it here."

"Yogi, huh? Seems like a good fit for you."

Franklin laughed.

We leaned onto the bar, watching the three female bartenders. After a moment one of them broke free, putting her boot up on something behind the bar and throwing a hand on her hip.

"Well, look at you two," she said. Blonde hair was pulled into pigtails under a white cowboy hat. "You're obviously brothers."

"And you're obviously a cowgirl," Franklin replied.

"Only the New York City version of one, darlin'." She winked. Her belly was exposed from the tops of her low-hipped jeans to her tied-off green-and-white plaid shirt. She took on an exaggerated analytical look. "Let me guess." She looked at Franklin. "You're a model."

"He's the model," Franklin said, nodding toward me. "You'll be seeing his face in Times Square in a month, so get a good look at it now."

"Bullshit," the girl responded instantly, her hand dropping off her hip.

"Thanks," I said as Franklin laughed.

"Believe what you want," he said, "but he's going to be the next big thing. Was discovered right here in the city."

She looked suspiciously at me. The hand went back to its hip.

"How about five Buds?"

"You got it, doll," she said, cracking her gum for emphasis. A moment later she was back with five longnecks. She unholstered a bottle opener from a back pocket, popping them open in quick succession and sending the bottle caps careening toward the back of the bar.

"He's actually an author, this one," Franklin said. "Damn talented one at that."

"If he's the author, what do you do? Sell cars?"

"Close. Aspiring game show host."

"Now *that* I believe," she said.

He pulled out a postcard that had one of his paintings on it, and on the back the address for his upcoming solo show. He slid it across the bar, and she took the card with both hands and read it.

"An artist."

"Oh gimme a break," I muttered.

She put it into the back pocket without the bottle opener. People were crowding around us, trying to get her attention. "Maybe I'll see you there."

"That would be great."

"Maybe before."

"What's your name?" His hand reached out and she dropped hers into it.

"Grace."

"Franklin," he responded. "This, as you have surmised, is my younger brother Logan, who will soon be a fixture, if not in Times Square, at least on the *New York Times* bestseller list."

She smiled and offered me a quick handshake — this one proper — before her attention went back to my brother.

"We got a thirsty crowd," Franklin said, handing me two beers while he took three. "Better get to 'em before they get angry."

"You're telling me?" She indicated the people around us.

"Talk to you later, Grace."

"See ya boys," she said, but her eyes never left Franklin.

As we took a few steps away from the bar, pushing shoulder-first through the crowd, I spoke into Franklin's ear. "How do you do it?"

"Do what?"

"Do what? Seriously? Fucking flirt. So easily."

Franklin glanced at me. "Its just conversation."

"No, man. I'm pretty good at conversation. What you do is something else entirely. I can't even explain it. Why didn't you just get her number?"

"Blondes aren't my type. Or bartenders. Or white girls. You know that."

"Oh come on."

"Besides, now she knows how to get hold of me."

"Yeah," I said, "but — but — " We came back to our group.

"It's a big city, Logan," Franklin said, putting the bottles on a high table top. "It's full of beautiful women."

"It's also full of hundred dollar bills, which doesn't help me a whole lot."

By midnight Hogs and Heifers was dense with people standing six deep at the bar. The smoke was so heavy it hung beneath the lights like low-lying clouds. Our group had managed to hold onto the pool table for most of the night, losing control only twice. I had switched from Budweiser to the much cheaper Pabst tall boys and had gained four extra ounces in the process, along with the likelihood of a much worse hangover.

"You know," Franklin said, after we'd been handily beaten by Carissa and Jackson, "there's a woman in my building. A neighbor. Really nice, and she happens to work for Random House — some kind of high level press thing or something. I forget exactly what her job is. But the three of us should go out when you get close to being done with your novel. She's cool, and if you pitch the book discreetly — well, who knows. It's worth a shot."

"Really?" A little drunk, I leaned awkwardly on the table. "That could be one of those once-in-a-lifetime things."

"In New York City, you'll find that once-in-a-lifetime opportunities come along about once a month, if you're paying attention. If you're gonna put up with the filth and the bullshit crime and the yellow summertime air while living in a shoebox for a grand a month, you might as well make the most of it."

I took a swig of beer and nodded. New York wisdom.

He looked at me, and I saw behind the blue of his eyes the consideration of something he'd decided to stuff.

"Just say it," I told him.

"I don't wanna bust your balls."

"Just fucking say it."

He sighed. "Well, you can write anywhere in the world, right? But if you're gonna write here you might as well use New York for what it's worth."

"I get that."

He nodded, but wasn't finished. "You look like a typical starving New York artist. Skin and bones strung together by hope and dressed in thrift." His blue eyes held mine. "It doesn't have to be that way."

"Jesus, Franklin." My anger flared. "Don't fucking hold back on my account." I then condescended back. "I can't afford three-hundred-fucking-dollar cowboy boots."

"It's not about the boots," he replied, patiently and without offense. "Look, I'm just calling it like I see it. I get it — it's a fucking shit show here. Tough adjustment, but fuck. Adjust, and then get to work."

"Hey man, I *have* been busting my ass. I *have* been working. I'm a fucking caterer living in the East Village. Should I be moving concrete?"

He laughed uncomfortably and looked away, taking a sip of his beer. "Let me try again. I'm not trying to pick a fight with you. I'm just telling you that I've been where you are, *exactly* where you are. I'm just reminding you that you chose this path because it means something — it means working, every day, to get what you want. You put in that work, the doors will open. Just a matter of time: work hard, have talent, success will follow. And," he looked me up and down and smiled, "I've got a bunch of clothes I'm getting rid of. I'll help you upgrade your wardrobe so you look less like an East Village cliché."

"You know what's great about *my* job," Jackson interrupted, putting a white sneaker up on the bottom rung of my stool. His shoulder-length brown hair made his head look too big for his body. A thin arm was thrown over my shoulder.

"Somehow I think you're about to tell me."

His teeth were like the Cheshire Cat's, huge and friendly and yet malevolent. "In the morning, car comes in — broken. In the afternoon, car goes out — fixed. Life. It can be simple like that. Honest day's work for an honest day's wages, you know? Why you wanna fuck around with this art shit, anyway? One artistic Downing brother is one too many."

"I honestly don't know," I replied, making him smile at the play on words.

"You been listening to your idiot brother too much. Listen to me, Logan: life don't gotta be tough. Couple a pretty boys like the two of yous — got the looks. Even have more than just shit for brains. Should go into sales, sit behind a desk, marry a pretty young thing, pop out some fuckin' kids, and let life come to you, man. Get your fucking check, get your fucking vacation, get your fucking pension, get your fucking old lady, retire, and die with a beer belly and money in the bank. Have some drinks and play some pool with your buds along the way. Easy, man. *Easy*." Jackson squeezed me with his skinny arm. "How old are you?"

"Twenty-one."

He nodded. "'Fore you know it you'll be thirty. I got started on a pension job at eighteen. At fifty, I'm out. Not even that old. Only twenty-two years from now."

"As long as I've been alive?"

"He's gonna fish," Franklin said, sarcastically. "And watch reruns."

Jackson smiled his huge smile and nodded. "That's *exactly* what I'm gonna do. *Exactly*. I'll be retired in twenty-two years while you two assholes will still be chasing fuckin' moonbeams and unicorns. Now let's get you Nancies on the table."

I looked at my watch: 3:00. We'd been in the bar for most of the night and I was very drunk. The crowd had thinned by half. I was shooting pool with Carissa and Franklin was leaning on the far end of the table.

"Don't you get no discount on Bud?" Jackson asked.

"Fuck. I don't work for beer," Franklin said.

"That was a big job, right? Billboards and shit?"

"Yeah."

Franklin had recently finished a freelance illustration job for Budweiser.

"Hey," I said, "how come you don't show your illustration? It's great work."

Franklin ran a hand through his short hair. "In the art world, you're considered a sellout if you do illustration *and* art. It's like a shit stain on your resume. Fucking bullshit pretentious nonsense."

"What's the objection to?"

"Commercializing. Like the fact that I have Budweiser and Heineken as clients means that I'll infect their gallery with corporate sponsorship. The same sponsorship that underwrites shows at museums, I might add."

"But you're not showing the paintings you did for illustration clients, are you?"

"Of course not. That's how I eat. The show is fine art."

I took the shot and missed. "Fuck." I handed to cue to Jackson.

"You're gonna lose," he whispered with a smile.

"Yeah yeah. Just fucking shoot. Who cares if you do both?" I asked Franklin. "Didn't Andy Warhol cross that bridge like thirty fucking years ago?"

Franklin nodded, emptying most of his beer. A waitress passed.

"Hey there," he said. "Two more Buds?"

"You got it, hon," she said.

"Pabst for me," I interjected. "Tall boy." Then, to Franklin, "Hey — you don't want to go and talk to the hot bartender again?" Franklin ignored my question and instead said, "Warhol had a particular genius.

Mainly that he fucked with the art establishment and especially around the ideas of so-called high art versus so-called low art."

"Didn't he say art is whatever you can get away with?"

Franklin shook his head. "No, some other fuckhead said it. But he might as well have. He perfected that idea, and we've been suffering for it ever since. Fucking postmodern art, man. A lot of Warhol's shit was interesting, daring even, though he produced a ton of turds. But those who've followed in his shoes? Fuck, man. Some of the most vapid, empty, narcissistic pile of collective garbage in the world. You wonder why no one buys fine art these days? Because no one knows what it is anymore. They buy a million dollar house and get their art at Ikea because the postmodernists burned the house to the ground."

I was just out of college and the contours of my freshman philosophy class were still surprisingly sharp. "Isn't it something like modernism is about critiquing society, postmodernism is about critiquing the whole system — including the artist himself?"

Jackson made a shot, a bank. "Told ya," he said. "You're going down, writer boy."

"Who knows, man," Franklin said, before immediately betraying himself. "Mainly, postmodernism is self-referencing and ironic, an inside joke about an inside joke. It's deconstructive."

Jackson missed his next shot. "Hey professors," he said, "what about the state of this fucking pool game? I'm getting my ass deconstructed over here."

"Being dominated like that," Franklin noted without changing the seriousness of his tone, "must remind you of home."

"It must be so hard," Jackson shot back, the wide grin expanding, "being a *true* ah-tist. You know, I get *my* art from my five-year old niece. Does these nice drawl-ings in crayon. I frame 'em and put 'em on my wall and tell everybody they're motherfuckin' Basquiats that were fifteen grand each."

Franklin nodded. "Basquiat was a genius, but your point is taken."

"Just come down to the dealership," Jackson said, "and get a *real* job."

"Because the world needs more mechanics," Franklin said.

"Yeah, what we *really* need is more art and ah-tists."

"I know you consider comics high art, Jackson," I said, trying to get in on the ribbing.

Jackson stepped in closer to me, pool cue in hand, smiling broadly. "I tell you what: I'll take a comic book any day over some fucking literary bullshit novel or fancy-pants art opening where they're showing green fucking triangles."

"You'll love my next show," Franklin said. "It's red fucking triangles. It's ironic."

"Fuck ironic," Jackson said. "Play some pool, you pretentious assholes."

"Franklin," Carissa called, throwing a balled-up napkin at him. "Your shot! Quit talking!"

"*Jesus!*" Jackson said when he turned around. "Just put me outta my fucking misery already, will ya? You're toying with me! Let's finish this game so we can get the art twins here to do something besides blowing hot air up each other's asses."

"I suppose," I said, looking across the table at my brother and smiling, "there's a lesson here in all of this. I just don't know what it is."

Wednesday

I look out at the parking lot full of cars from a bright orange table corralled by a black fence in downtown Denver. The outside seating of the Trudent offices is about four hundred square feet of concrete hemmed in by a few thin trees. I'm waiting for our CEO. My job today is to help him write an article for the *Harvard Business Review*, and by "help" I mean "write for him."

I know some writers who would bristle at letting someone take handed-off writing and call it their own, but for me it comes with the paycheck and stock options, and frankly it's more exciting than slogging through Salesforce, Uberflip, and Basecamp. If you don't know what those things are, I suggest you take a moment to fall to your god-loving knees and thank your creator.

"Logan," a deep and confident voice speaks from inside the building. I turn to see Michael on the phone, an index finger pointing up. "One moment — important call."

I nod. Michael is a tall man with short-cropped brown hair and small blue eyes. His head has a particular oblong shape. In skinny jeans and Converse, he's convincingly hip, even to my jaded eye.

He ends the call and sits down. "So you're the journalist, right?"

"Author."

He talks through my correction.

"So as a journalist I think you're the ideal person with the perfect skills to do this. I've been in this business for ten years." He is standing again by the fourth word, hands following his mouth like a conductor as he shifts from one foot to the other. He gives me a long, rambling, and occasional self-contradictory version of his vision for the company, which I dutifully capture.

Later at my desk, I write up the piece. It's straightforward. I plow through a first draft in just over an hour, then head outside to Broadway and stand looking absent-mindedly east, the sun at my back. A woman walks past. This stranger has dark hair that falls heavily on her shoulders, and in a flash I remember the first time I met my fiancée, almost three years back. I had been standing in line in a coffee shop looking at the perfect-fitting jeans of a woman in front of me, with hair that looked like it came out of a shampoo commercial.

"I'll take a coconut milk, decaf cappuccino," the voice said from a face I couldn't see.

"Sure thing," replied the barista, and then looked around her to me. "Something started for you?"

"Coffee, black, as big as you've got, for here."

"That's sixteen ounces."

"Beautiful."

"I'm going to get his real quick," the barista said to the woman in front of me.

"Sorry," I smiled, as she turned. She was slender and composed. She smiled back. "That's okay. My order is a lot more high maintenance."

I nodded. "Perhaps these drinks are metaphors."

She gave an awkward laugh that seemed incongruent with her poise. I stepped around her to pay, unable to think of anything else to say, then turned to look for a seat.

Two girls in yoga pants were at one table, a bearded kid with a gigantic PC occupied a table for four, and the double tables were taken by men with man buns, women in festival wear, and a handful who looked like they might actually have real jobs and not be living off of loans, their parents' trusts, or both. The north-facing wall was large and mostly glass, looking out over a parking lot and a stretch of blue sky. A few trees leaned into view. The floor was concrete, local art hung on the walls. There was one open two-top against the north-facing window. I took it, facing out, and debated whether or not I wanted to pull my computer from my bag or get up and grab a weekly newspaper.

"Excuse me?"

I started, surprised. She gave another awkward laugh. "Sorry!"

"No," I said, delighted, "don't be sorry."

"Do you mind if I join you? There aren't any other open tables."

"Of course!"

She sat down, demurely, knees tucked tightly into each other. She looked at her drink.

"Do you have work you need to do?"

"Nothing that can't wait," I replied. "Do you?"

She shook her head. "I have a massage in twenty minutes. I'm early so I stopped here to kill the time."

"How far is the massage place?"

"About five minutes."

"Could be awkward," I said, relieved to have finally found a joke somewhere in there.

"I brought a book," she parried, "just in case." We both laughed.

Her skin was tan and smooth; eyebrows delicately arched over light brown eyes, nose the kind I imagined snooty girls asked their plastic surgeons to imitate — narrow and noble. The more I looked at her, the more I saw just how perfectly her features worked together.

"So what do you do?" she asked.

"What?"

"Do. You. Do."

"Right," I flushed, looking down at my hands. They held no advice. "Well, I'm a freelance writer." I looked back up.

"Oh?" Genuine curiosity. "What kind of writing?" She was wearing a grey top that looked like wool, some kind of wrap tossed over her right shoulder. She adjusted it.

"Just advertising stuff. Marketing. Web."

She looked at me with curiosity. "Why do I think that's your cover story?"

That caught me completely off guard, and I laughed more in surprise than humor. In a different city the comment would have been said with a wry smile, an intellectual lob into my court to see if I could volley it back, but she said it as a sincere observation.

I mumbled something incoherent.

"You don't have to answer," she demurred.

"No," I rushed, our eyes meeting, "it's just a complicated story for a woman heading to a massage in — " I pulled out my phone and opened it up to check the time.

"Woah," she said. "Still with the flip phone!"

Another flush on my end. "Oh," I said. "I'm waiting for the next one to come out. iPhone that is. Four."

"I get it. I lived in Spain for years and only ever had a flip. I just got the three myself, and I'm not into tech that much, but I don't know I ever lived without it. It's kinda cool you still have a flip phone." She looked embarrassed.

I nodded. "So we don't have much time, but you asked me a sincere question and I want to attempt a sincere answer. In like six minutes." I decided to jump in with both feet. "I wrote a book a bunch of years ago and it got published by a big publisher and made some money — "

"Really?"

I nodded. "And the truth is, I've been in a creative rut ever since and am not certain if I can get my third book out of my head or not."

"What happened to the second one?"

"DOA." I paused. "Well, truth here. Not DOA. I wasted a ton of money self-publishing it, which was a huge mistake because it wasn't good enough for a publisher, and I should have gotten that message, but I didn't. I recycled the copies that didn't sell and buried the idea and the book."

"That seems rash."

I laughed. "Yeah. Maybe that wasn't so smart. Anyway, I freelance so I have time to create and work on book number three."

"That sounds pretty great."

"Some days it is. And some days it's not. It's not always an easy existence, although it does mean I can be hanging out in coffee shops at two in the afternoon." I was sweating a little and wiped my forehead with my fingers.

"It's not easy following your own path," she observed.

"No," I agreed, "it is not."

"But — follow your heart and the money will follow it."

"That's what they told me too. But I'm not sure the universe has gotten the memo." I took a sip of my coffee. "I used half of our six minutes. What about you?"

"I'm a coach."

I nodded. "And why do I think that's your cover story?"

She laughed. "Touché. I'm halfway though my first book. About women in the workplace. The shattering of the patriarchy. But, see? That's too simple. The patriarchy has done a lot for us women, which most don't want to acknowledge, and it's created a ton of problems for us. And for men."

"No shit?"

She nodded.

"What else?"

The awkward laugh. "I want to expand my business online so I can take the coaching model but scale it up many times. Virtual courses, work — all around feminine empowerment, but not by making women just men-light, but guiding women into their own unique places of power and insight."

"That's awesome. What else?"

"Keep traveling the world. Move around. Find a man. Get hitched. Have a kid."

"That seems pretty clear. Time line?"

She bit the corner of her left lip. "I dunno. I've got time, but I don't want to feel rushed about it, you know?"

"Never want to rush a baby."

"You?"

"Oh, I rush babies all the time. I'm on number three."

"Really?"

"No."

She gave me a tight-lipped, friendly shake of her head.

I smiled. "I guess the truth is I've never much thought about family or kids. Too involved with my own path, which is probably not the best admission."

A little laugh.

"So I have like another thousand questions for you, but I know you have to go and get a massage, and every minute I keep you is another minute you're not getting bodywork. Is there any chance you might want to continue this conversation over dinner or drinks or more coconut frappuccinos?"

"There's no such thing as a frappuccino," she corrects, standing. "But yes, I'd like that."

"Can I get your number?" I laughed. "And, uh, your name?" We introduced ourselves and exchanged numbers, and then I watched her walk out to her car. She looked back at me once, smiling.

I realize I've been standing on the corner through three or four changes of the traffic light and shake off the unwelcome memory. I walk back to the company building, through the open-planed office to the kitchen. I help myself to one of the complimentary Cokes and a bowlful of trail mix. I sit at a high table, thumbing through my phone. Jamie walks by.

"Hey," I say as she passes, barely looking up. She stops.

"Hey. So," she says directly, "Jen told me you had a book published."

I put my phone down. "Yes. But it was a long time ago."

She looks at me over the tops of her glasses. "That's impressive."

"Is it?" I really don't know anymore.

She nods. "No, it's impressive. What's it about?"

"The book?" I ask, stupidly. The look she gives me seems to agree with my self-assessment.

"Right. Well, I wrote it when I was a lot younger. It's a story set in the suburbs, kind of a dark coming of age story that involves things not being what they seem. It's actually kind of violent. I was trying to show, at the time, that under the bright veneer of suburban middle-class life there was also a darkness, and that things weren't as great as they looked on the surface. For all the strife and struggle of the inner cities, the suburbs sometimes hid their own worlds of suffering."

She lifts an eyebrow over the rim of the glasses. "So you wrote it from experience."

I laugh. "You don't miss much, do you?"

"No. Do you still write, aside from what you do here?"

I shrug. "Sometimes." She raises both eyebrows at this. "I am writing now, a little. Actually about those days. And about things now. But it's just for me. There's not much money in art."

She looks thoughtful. "I appreciate art. But I appreciate money too. Money more." Seeing as Jamie is maybe thirty-two or thirty-three and already in a director-level position, I have no doubts about that. "What brought you to Trudent?"

"The people. The corporate culture. The youth of the team."

Her eyes stare like a detective's.

"The stock and the money helped," I add. "A lot."

A wry smile. "Tech just has more financial opportunity than regular companies, and this one is solid. It's all about results, so that your hard work is rewarded with more than a *pension*." She sort of sneers that last word. She looks around the office. "Yeah, the people here are okay and so is the culture, but if I really want those things I'll get a job at non-profit. The work is dull, but so what?"

"It *is* dull," I nod. "Especially when you have to write about it."

"Yeah, I bet. I don't envy you. You freelanced your whole life, right?"

"Just about."

"Must be quite a switch," she observes.

I consider that. "Some days are tougher than others, but you get the hang of it."

"Well," she says, taking half a step away. "You're obviously a novice in being part of a team, but your writing is pretty stellar."

She walks off before I can respond.

Winter, 1995

It looks like a baroque museum exploded," I said as we stepped inside. I shook off the New York City cold that had worked itself between my coat and clothes.

"I sure as shit didn't pick the place," Franklin replied. "She's said she'd be in the back."

It was a midtown restaurant thick in gold leaf and white marble. Huge porcelain vases stood like sentries around the perimeter, sprouting immense collections of dried flowers from tables laced in gilded carvings. Antique mirrors reflected the room back to itself from veined glass.

I chewed on my lip as we walked through. I was wearing my brother's hand-me-down clothes — his jeans, rolled up because he was taller than me, and a black collared shirt with red lacing. I had rebelled against his suggestion that I borrow a shiny pair of shoes and instead wore my battered combat boots.

The bar was to our right, white marble and gold trim with black finish, stretching far enough to seat fifteen people. The high tables closest to the street were taken, full of middle-aged women and men dressed for a night of theater or music. The formal dining area was behind a half wall with two of the giant custodial vases on either side. We ducked between as though gaining entrance into a kingdom. A woman at a four-top waved energetically.

"Franklin!" she stood to plant kisses on both his cheeks. "*So* nice to see you!" She stepped back, holding his hands in hers for a moment and looking into his eyes. "You look great!"

"So do you, Rebecca."

She turned to me. She had tightly spiraled brown hair and lipstick that made me think of fire engines and red chilis. "*This* must be your brother."

She was tiny, not more than five-foot-two or more than a hundred pounds, but took up space the way only a lifelong New Yorker can. She offered me her hand on a straight arm and gave a hard, firm shake.

"I've heard a lot about you."

"Franklin is a good cheerleader," I admitted, smiling.

"Aw, that's so sweet. You guys really look out for each other?"

We both nodded.

"So sit *sit*!" she said, gesturing to the small booth. "It's so nice to see you! Both!"

She and Franklin immediately started talking about the weather — it was getting cold — and a recent doorman strike, which allowed me time to settle in.

A tattooed waitress, pale and purpled-haired and wearing an altered wedding dress, stopped by.

"Drinks?" she mumbled in a tone barely loud enough to be heard.

"Scotch, rocks," Franklin said. "Oban."

"Do you have a nice Barbera?" Rebecca asked.

"We have one from Monferrato people seem to like," the waitress sighed.

"Sounds great."

The server looked at me. I hadn't yet acquired a taste for straight alcohol, but needed something much stronger than wine.

"Margarita," I said, ending the word in a question. I saw Franklin make a kind of face.

"We only do coin style," the waitress said.

"Sure," I replied, having no idea what that meant.

"What kind of tequila?"

I only knew Jose Cuervo, of course, being recently out of college, but Franklin jumped in.

"Give him Mañana Añejo," he said. "In some ways," continued Franklin, wrapping up the small talk that had started before, "I like it when the doormen are on strike. I don't have to think about what to say before I come into my building, and it's not like it's that hard to open a door."

Rebecca wore a beautifully fitted leather coat whose orange-brown color was reminiscence of the seventies with a purple scarf thrown around her neck. Green corduroys tucked themselves into black boots.

"Well," she said, a fingernail, painted a rich red that matched her lips, carefully scratching at the tip of her nose, "I agree, but as a woman it's nice to come back and have a doorman there to open the door and not make you feel like you have to start looking over your shoulder a block from your building." Her cheeks were narrow and her chin tapered, her cool grey-blue eyes warm and curious.

Franklin nodded. "Good point."

The drinks came and Rebecca turned to me. "So Logan. Where do you live?"

"Fourteenth and A," I said.

"Oh, across from Stuyvesant Town."

"Block down."

"Colorful over there," she observed.

"That's one way to put it," I laughed. "That's how a realtor would sell it, at least. It's a little intense but it's cheap and it's never, ever uninteresting."

"Great place for a young writer to live," said Franklin, sipping his scotch.

Rebecca lifted her wine glass. "Tell me your impressions of the city. I'm always curious what new people think."

That question sat between us like the opening salvo of a job interview. "Well," I started, "I actually just wrote about it recently."

Rebecca raised her eyebrows and waited. I noticed how loud and busy the restaurant was. I reminded myself there was no pressure; this was just conversation.

I cleared my throat and sat forward. "I was going over to 7Bs the other night, not even that late. I was walking down Seventh, right across from Tompkins. There were these three junkies hunkered down between two cars, and I happened to stop and look when this woman stabbed a needle between her fingers and injected herself."

"Tompkins." Rebecca shook her head.

"They should just pave that park over," Franklin said.

"So, you know, I'm not a New Yorker, and I stare. She looks up at me and screeches *What are you looking at?* and starts to get up, and I just take off, straight to the bar."

Rebecca nodded politely.

I finished the rest of my drink in one swallow. The waitress was walking past and I shook the glass at her. "I mean, the junkies. They're kind of impressive, right? No more social status to bog them down — they've transcended race or gender with their addiction, and they have this admirable devotion to getting high, no matter the cost."

She nodded, closed her right hand into a fist, and leaned her chin onto it.

"But it's the failed and failing artists who are the most interesting."

"How do you know they're artists?"

I shrugged. "I listen."

She nodded. "Go on."

"I mean, I dunno. Maybe it takes one to know one. They're too old to break through, right? But they've been at it too long to do anything else. You can see it in their eyes, in the stiff way they hold themselves, like a left hook might come from anyone at anytime. Not quite broken, but not much fight left in them either, except the tired fight of defiance."

I glanced at my brother's drink with envy, resolving to acquire a taste for scotch.

"Please, continue," she said. Franklin sat back.

"The Village — the East Village — is like a weird kind of purgatory, you know? I mean, the projects with all those poor and disenfranchised people. The Chinese and Korean and Indian immigrants, struggling to make a dime with their businesses. The junkies. I think if people find success there, they move out to greener pastures uptown or across town. And I can't help but imagine how hard it is to be the forty-five-year-old musician or comedian or writer sleeping on a blowup mattress in some crappy flat on Avenue B, surrounded by crime and desperation and the failed dreams of their youth."

She glanced at Franklin, then turned to me, her hand coming away from her chin. "Logan, I've never heard it described in quite that way."

I blushed. "Too judgmental? It might be way off," I said, backpedaling. "What do I know? I just moved there!"

"No no," she laughed. "I think you're onto something."

"Oh," I said, too shocked to continue.

"Well," Franklin said, "if you're not sure if you're right, just report on what happens to me in a decade."

They both laughed.

The waitress set my drink down. "Can I get you guys any food?"

"Yeah," Franklin said, "I'm starving."

We ordered and the waitress took our menus.

"So Rebecca, what's new in the biz?" Franklin asked.

"New?" she said with a laugh. "You have no idea. Crazy."

"What's going on?"

"Biggest change in the book business in a generation. I think the best way I can sum it up is I'm always on the cusp of either getting fired or promoted." She lowered her voice to create a sense of urgency and secrecy. "It's these new box stores. Have you heard of Borders?"

"Logan was just talking about that."

Rebecca leaned in. "They're starting to put a lot of pressure on the smaller, independent bookstores, which is realigning our distribution channels and, frankly, our sales and marketing strategies." She looked at both of us. "We're moving away from the mom and pop stores and to a more corporate and streamlined business. It's great for us, honestly. I'm not sure it will be great in the long run though."

She turned to me. "Small bookstore owners hate Borders, of course. It's putting a ton of pressure on them, and it's expected to drive a lot of them out of business. The age of the independent bookstore might be at the beginning of its end."

"I like the quirky little bookstores," I said, "but they never have a wide variety of books. I love Borders because they can afford to carry so many kinds. I can lose myself in one for hours. And the magazines. And coffee. I dunno, maybe that makes me a sellout artist or something, but I like them."

Rebecca nodded, then turned back to Franklin. "The jury's out whether they'll be good for authors. They'll likely put more pressure on publishers to create blockbusters at the expense of more esoteric work," she shrugged, then put a hand on Franklin's arm. "But that's the way of the world, I suppose. So, Franklin, what's new with *you*?"

"The solo show two months ago did well — "

"So sorry I couldn't come! I was in London."

I knew that Franklin's show hadn't gone well. No paintings had been sold, though there had been a lot of interest. His finances weren't much better than mine, and I wondered how he managed to always seem above the fray.

"No problem. I have another solo show in DC this summer and then another one back here in New York in the fall."

"Three solo shows in a year? Look at you! When's the one in DC?"

"July nineteenth."

Rebecca whipped out her purse and pulled out a planner, flipping through the pages. "You know," she said, "I'm actually free then. I'm gonna put it down! That would be so fun!"

"I'll get a good crew together," Franklin said with a smile. "It'll be an epic party."

"And the illustration?"

"Great. It's hard to keep up with the commercial work."

"Good for you. I have a couple of book projects coming up that might benefit from your particular style," she said. "I'll give you a call next week. You should come in and we can talk about them. We'll let Random House buy us lunch."

Franklin smiled. "Thursday is open for me."

"Come by my office about noon," she said. Then, to me: "Franklin tells me you're working on a novel."

Her directness and change of subject caught me completely off guard. I almost asked *What?* but caught myself, nodding instead.

"Wonderful. What kind of writing?"

I exhaled, taking a drink of my sugary margarita. "Literary. Literary fiction," I said, leaning unnaturally on my elbow.

"That's *wonderful*," Rebecca said, almost before the words had come out of my mouth, looking from me to Franklin. "You would think being surrounded by writers all day, every day, that I might have picked something up. But I just don't have the soul of an artist, I'm afraid. Working with them is the next best thing. Good for you for jumping into a novel, Logan. That takes real courage."

I nodded, ready to go on, but she changed the subject again, as she and Franklin started down the path of New York City politics.

They were talking about the new mayor, Rudy Giuliani, as I mentally prepared to tell Rebecca about the novel. *It's a modernist tale, set in the suburbs of the eighties. It follows the kind of everyday evil that can live inside of the well-groomed houses we pass, most days, with people we know really only through waving at them from inside our cars.* But their conversation deepened, moving onto an Italian art exhibition at the Met and from there, inexplicably, to the O.J. Simpson trial that was underway.

Two hours later, the three of us, well fed and a little tipsy, stood in front of the restaurant. The streets were hushed and the night cold, that particular kind of chill that funnels down the tall buildings and right into the neck of your coat. I pushed my hands far into my pockets.

"It was great seeing you," Rebecca said, giving Franklin a hug.

"You too," he replied.

"*So* nice to catch up. And lunch Thursday!"

"Can't wait."

"And," she turned and smiled. "It was nice meeting *you*, Logan." She held out her hand and I dug mine out of my pocket.

"You too."

As she walked away, she paused, narrow face turned to profile. "Logan — send me that manuscript when you're done with it. Franklin has my work address. Just send it care of me. I'll pass it along to my people." She pulled a purple knitted cap down firmly onto her head before strutting off at a New York City pace.

Something struck my shoulder and I took a stumbling step to recover my balance before realizing Franklin had just punched me.

"Dude!" he exclaimed.

And just like that, a once-in-a-lifetime opportunity happened, and what had been an idealistic dream was now in the realm of the possible.

Winter, 1995

The bathroom was tiny, even by New York City standards. It had a half-sized tub and a sink barely big enough to wash one's hands. When standing, my head was only a few inches from the aggressively lumpy popcorn finish ceiling, which looked as if it would easily remove the hair and scalp of a slightly taller and less cautious person.

I leaned my back against the free wall next to the sink, feet propped on the toilet. Carissa was watching TV in the other room. When I had last seen her, she was curled into a cat-like ball on the couch with just her eyes and freckles sticking out. In the past I had tried to read next to her but my attention would get drawn toward the TV and an hour would pass with my book uselessly spread open to my nostrils.

It was strangely cozy for a bathroom, even with the small, eight-inch-wide window above the toilet that opened into an area, like a giant chimney, running up the inside of the building to the roof. I suppose it was there to let some kind of breeze flow through but, as I was on the first floor, I mostly got oddly disquieting smells and gloomy shadows even at midday.

I turned the page and shifted on the tile floor. I was reading David Foster Wallace's *Infinite Jest*, which had just been released. Postmodern literature sometimes had the effect of making me feel like there was a party where everyone was talking and laughing and having a good time except for me. I fought through another four pages before I set the book down, temporarily defeated.

I sipped from the cup of tea next to me and my gaze fell onto the cover. Its most prominent feature was the author's name, with puffy clouds in a blue sky that partially obscured the book's title. Wallace had become a newfound celebrity — the heir apparent to the postmodern emeritus chair of literature, then squatted on by Thomas Pynchon. I had managed to track four novels in Wallace's one. There was a sports story about tennis, a coming-of-age tale of addicts in a halfway house, a weird conceit about a lethally entertaining video, and finally the story of a former singer who became president of the United States and decided to alter its borders in a very peculiar way.

Like so many postmodern books, a singular narrative had been deconstructed and Wallace seemed to have made no attempt to put things into a format that could be easily followed. It made my occasional habit of drinking wine and reading particularly perilous, for two glasses of wine would sufficiently dim my wits to prevent me from following the story. I sipped my caffeinated tea again.

I flipped the book over and halfheartedly read the fawning endorsements from magazines and other writers. Wallace was famous, wealthy, and established while still a relatively young man. He'd been climbing the ladder of success ever since his first book came out a decade before, although I wondered if the fact that both of Wallace's parents were established professors and his own time at Harvard had helped. The *Times*, the *New Yorker*, NPR, and other national presses seemed to favor writers who, like Wallace, had the pedigree of prestigious schools behind them, perhaps through established lines of communication between elite universities and elite publications and reviewers. Or maybe because of old-fashioned nepotism. Or maybe because elites just took care of each other behind the façade of the American meritocracy. But there I was, reading on the floor of a bathroom and with a lifeline to a major publisher, through nothing more than dumb luck. Maybe Wallace had just been as stupidly lucky as I.

My book, still without a title, wasn't progressive. It wasn't cutting edge. It was stubbornly modern in its writing and approach, with too much care for the reader and too little desire to deconstruct the narrative form. Wallace, by contrast, didn't seem to give a fuck about the reader. He was more preoccupied with his own writing, his love of wordplay and erudition, his mastery of language, and whatever flow he might be in on a particular day. The book was more of a heap of words than a story and yet Wallace was, unquestionably, a master. No matter how hard I tried, each time I read a page of his writing I couldn't find the heart to begrudge his success. Genius, after all, isn't easily dismissed with pettiness.

I took another mouthful of tea, unsure whether I wanted to climb back into Wallace's mind again or abandon him to what sounded like *ER* in the other room. I could hear actors breathlessly delivering lines. I stood and placed my palms on the ceiling, elbows bent, and stretched. Listening, I heard the unmistakable baritone of Doctor Doug Ross: "I dedicated my *life* to pediatric medicine, to kids in agony and pain. Ricky Abbot was *going to die*, not in a month, or week, or days, but in *hours*. *Nothing* I could have done would have changed that."

I smiled: *Ricky Abbott.* That came from Made-Up Sounding Names for TV.

The strikingly handsome and mildly tortured Dr. Ross was explaining that it was sometimes impossible to save a kid but damn it — *damn* it — it *was* possible to save him from suffering and give him a little dignity. I couldn't resist his sonorous earnestness. I left the bathroom to sit down next to Carissa, still buried up to her chin in a blanket. Her eyes were moist, fixed on Dr. Ross's tanned face.

"What going on?"

"*Shhh!*"

I sat quietly, and she whispered very loudly, "I'll fill you in in a sec."

Wednesday Night

Sounds like a tough day," she says to me over dinner. We're eating roasted chicken and some asparagus that, if I'm honest, I admit I've overcooked. I stab a strand, which flaccidly collapses around my fork.

I nod. "I've had better." Then, changing the subject, "How's the marketing writing going?"

"Pretty good. Got the first draft of the story down. I'll send it to you to edit if that's okay." She's wearing burgundy corduroys and a white top that's cut high in the front. Her feet are bare and under the table I can see the green shade of her pedicure. Her hair is pulled back into a ponytail. She looks tired tonight, heaviness weighing down the skin around her eyes.

"Sure."

"Looking to launch on Monday."

I nod. It's early evening, but we've moved into very late fall and the sunlight has long left us. We're at our rectangular table in a house so quiet it's nearly solemn.

"Can I share something with you?"

"Of course."

"It's about our engagement and wedding."

I nod my head and then, after a pause, look up. We were engaged half a year before, in Sebastopol, California.

"I know we agreed that a temporary ring would be okay," she says, spinning the gold and faux diamond ring around her finger. "I know you're in a lot of debt, and working hard now, and not really liking your job. And this ring was a couple of hundred bucks."

I nod and put the overcooked asparagus in my mouth.

"It's just ... I want a *real* ring. A ring that's not just a placeholder. Something that means ... something. That costs something, that I'll —

that we'll — have for the rest of our lives. I know you're trying to get your finances under control," she continues almost as an apology. "I know you're working really hard, and you're not happy. But you're not really saving, and I know your credit is maxed out, so it just seems like it's something that's not going to happen."

I nod again. My jaw macerates the stalk into something like paste. I drink some wine to wash it down.

"I appreciate that you're taking a more adult path to life. Otherwise we're never going to get married or start a family."

There was a time in the very recent past when it seemed that marriage and family and a secure job would be an island of sanity. The artist's life is a sea of chaos, one I'd sailed for too many years already. Then I'd found this beautiful and sensitive being, slender but strong, with luxurious brown hair falling halfway down her back. She had a paleness that reminded me of the coolness of marble. Only the skin around her eyes gave away her true age and the pressure she often felt; the skin there sometimes looked as thin as parchment. She was smart and ambitious and well read, and in the end I had fallen head-over-heels in love with her. When I turned my back on my writing, it had seemed like the wisest and most mature decision I'd made in years, maybe ever.

"That's true," I replied.

We sit for a long time without speaking, as we do a lot these days. "I've been thinking about Carissa," I say, surprising her almost as much as I surprise myself. I seldom mention Carissa, given what happened. But there it is between us, like a spilled glass of wine running toward the edge of the table.

She doesn't move. Her eyes are cast downward. She is considering her words, I can tell. She looks from her food to my glass of wine, then to the flickering candle, then to my fork, and then finally to me. Her face is a question mark.

"I'm writing again," I confess. "Just nights. Sometimes on weekends. Nothing much."

The left side of her mouth twitches and she bites at it, holding her lower lip in her teeth for a brief moment, gaze momentarily dropping.

"You said you were done with writing." Her words are cool, flat, as dispassionate as a museum curator's and as carefully chosen. "You said you were going to put writing aside for one full year, make money, and then we'd see — you'd see — if it was something you were really passionate about, or if it was just a kind of story you'd become enrolled in."

"I did say that," I agree, feeling myself withdrawing from her even though I don't move at all.

She looks down again, briefly, gathering the words into an obvious question. "So why are you writing?"

"I've just been writing about the old days," I say, "in New York City. A million years ago. When this all got set in motion. About Carissa. And Franklin — all of them, all of it. And a little about what's happening now. It's what I've been doing at night. Why I'm not coming to bed with you."

She raises an eyebrow.

"I know," I say. "And I've been drinking more than normal and I know you hate the smell. But the writing is helping me understand where things are now, I think. It's not to get published or anything," I say, feeling like a shield has been torn away from me.

She seems to hold her breath. "I understand," she breathes at last, "that you get ... " she searches for the word. "*Nervous* about getting married. Anybody would be who's been through what you did." Her eyes find mine, and I'm surprised at the tenderness in them. "It was horrible, I know, and the fact that you never talk about it tells me how much it's still inside of you. I know you miss her. That you love her, still. I hated that for a long time, but I understand it now. It's part of your soul that

I see and love. And I know you miss the writing." Her eyes glance at the candles burning between us. "But Logan." She looks back. "Carissa was a lifetime ago. Those stories are full of pain and hurt."

"Triumph, too," I snap. "And love."

She takes another long and thoughtful pause that makes me wish we could sometimes just fight, shout and scream and throw plates instead of being so fucking polite all the time, so fucking measured. "Sure," she says, reasonably. "But that life is ... " her sentence stumbles, but I know the word that trips her.

"Over," I say, but she shakes her head.

"In *transition*," she offers. "This is *our* life, yours *and* mine. Two are always stronger than one. You can't be a starving artist *and* building a stable life and family. It's just not possible. You can't be in love with someone else *and* in love with me. Something has to give to make room for us, fully. And I'm not willing to pay the cost of you staying with your old dreams and your old love. I've told you that since the beginning."

"I know," I say, and I do. "You've been very clear."

"So ... " She eases the words out. "You did promise that you wouldn't write for one year."

"I know."

"But ... I understand ... it's helping you come into greater clarity?"

I nod. "And I know you want a real ring," I concede. "And you deserve one."

A thoughtful pause, perhaps measuring the veracity of my words. "Okay." We sit for another moment. "I need to get ready for bed," she says at last, with a glance to the clock. We clear the plates silently and do the dishes together, also without speaking. Once we've cleaned up, she goes upstairs. We go through our routine: once she's in bed, I lie next to her and she talks a little about her day and her business. I'm rubbing her feet.

"Why don't you just lie here with me," she says in a voice that sounds young, vulnerable. "Instead of going downstairs."

"It's 8:30," I say with a laugh. "I'd love for us to go out and get a glass of wine together."

"I know, but you know I can't stay up late … or put alcohol in my system anymore." She smiles. "And I'm already in my jammies *and* in bed."

"Right."

I know I should get into bed with her, forget the writing for the night and the dreams lost and Carissa and the whisky downstairs and just fucking lie there, at least long enough for her to fall asleep against me, like in the early days. Feel her warmth against my body, her breath on my neck, the slender power that's present even in her sleeping body. But I don't.

"It's too early for me to get into bed." The voice sounds foreign to me. Hard.

"Okay." In that single word I hear the depth of her hurt and the size of the growing chasm between us. She turns away from me. "I love you," she says to the wall. "Good night."

I go to the door and linger, looking at the hair splayed across the pillow, illuminated in a column of light falling in from the hallway, then pull the door gently shut.

Spring, 1996

We were in a small bar in SOHO that cleared out the dining tables after nine to make a dance floor. Carissa was next to me. Both of us were watching the few people dancing. Her hair had bright pink highlights she'd put in just a few nights before. She wore a black shirt that that came in tight at her waist and a loose, floor-length skirt that showed her pink Converses whenever she crossed her legs.

"So," I said to her, "I finished the second draft last night."

"You did? Logan! That's awesome! How is it?"

"Fucked if I know."

She kicked me.

"Ow!"

"Fuck you don't know," she growled. "How is it?"

"I think it's pretty good," I laughed. "But don't hold me to that. It could be like the pride of a parent."

"Based on obligation not merit?"

I laughed at how easily she finished my sarcastic observations. "Exactly. She might be an ugly little simple-minded child, but she's *my* child and I'm proud of her."

"Good for you, Rocky," she said. "And you know what? You did pretty good for an aspiring writer."

"Oh *ha*."

"Too bad this is just the second round," she continued, her green eyes looking at the ceiling. "Fourteen more to go, and then we'll still have to wait for the decision."

"And at that point I'll be a middle-aged caterer chasing the dreams of his youth."

"Oh, I'm sorry," she said. "Did I say 'we'? I meant 'you,' since you'll obviously be single then." She smiled sweetly.

"Oh, I don't know," I said. "I might be the catering *manager* by then, pulling down something in the low-five figures. I think the ladies will be plenty impressed with a middle-aged man clinging to his youth. And I'll dye my hair. What's left of it."

"You're making me hot, baby, with all that talk of failure and middle age and bald spots." She slinked in next to me. "Besides, if you become a famous author, my days of making fun of your insecurities are numbered." Carissa's pink and brown hair in dual pigtails gave her a maliciously youthful look, like the evil sidekick of a supervillain.

"I'm going to get another round," I said. She put her hand on my arm.

"Hey — kidding aside, I'm proud of you, and it's sexy as hell. I love you."

I felt myself blush, which was a strange feeling with someone I knew so well and loved so much and never got embarrassed around. I smiled at her, then went for two shots and two more beers. We downed them as the bar began to fill up and the music deepened, making it harder to talk.

Carissa leaned into my ear. "I want to dance with you tonight."

I laughed.

"I'm serious," she said, pushing one of the pigtails off her shoulder. "I want you out there." Her green eyes were full of a mischievous fire. I was suddenly nervous looking at her, like we were on our second date and I wanted to impress her.

"Get out of here," I dismissed, laughing again, uncomfortably. "You know I can't dance."

"Logan, you're dancing with me tonight to celebrate your book."

"Absurd." I pounded my beer. "I'm going to get another drink while you think about how ridiculous the thought of me on a dance floor really is."

I ordered another beer and surveyed the small place. The bar looked like a diner, with booths and tables and cozy lights, opening up into what normally was additional seating but was now the dance floor. A DJ was in a corner opposite me, a large man with ebony skin, sleeve tattoos running down both arms, and wrap-around sunglasses. There were thirty or so people dancing. As my eyes swept back from them, they caught on Carissa with her pink and brown hair, tight top, and slinky skirt. Her beauty surprised me, probably because she had always been my buddy, my friend, and in a strange way I didn't often see her as a sexual object. I watched her small face and bright eyes tracking the room.

I got my drink and went back to the table.

"Okay," she said, having to shout. "You've had your drinks. Let's go dance."

"No."

"Don't be a killjoy. Come on."

"Baby, I can't dance," I protested. "You know this. We've done weddings. You dance. I drink."

"Nonsense," she stood and grabbed my hands. "Come on. I'll show you."

"Carissa ... "

"Shush. Come on!"

The only dancing I'd ever done had been at high school events, voluntarily gender segregated socials where the boys stood in tight packs for protection as the girls danced in nervous circles. The few boys brave enough to dance were scrutinized for any weaknesses in technique that might be weaponized against them, which I knew all too well from the few times I attempted to dance in what felt like a borrowed body.

Carissa successfully pulled me into the middle of the dance floor and started to move. She grinned. "You're adorable," she shouted in my ear. "It's not that bad. Look, you know the place you go in your writing?" She tapped her head.

I nodded. "Sure."

I felt her lips brush against my ear as she talked. "Go to that place, but go there in your body instead of your mind. Express yourself the same way." I took her hand and twirled her, awkwardly, grabbing the small of her back and pulling her close enough to smell her neck and the rush of her breath.

"That's it," she encouraged with a laugh, stepping in and playfully away. I swooped around behind her and took her fully in my arms, hands coming up just under her breasts, feeling her breath pumping in and out.

"Yes! That's it!"

I stumbled across her feet but laughed and her hands found my thighs, and then we parted again, turning and spinning as she giggled. The next time I pulled her to me, I kissed her, stopping our movement to make out in the middle of the dance floor like a couple of high school kids.

"You're doing great — don't think, just move."

And I did, thrilled at the ability of my body to actually find a rhythm. I didn't give a fuck what I looked like. After thirty minutes, my shirt was stuck to my back and my pants wet with sweat and I was grinning uncontrollably.

"I gotta pee," I mouthed to her, heading toward one of the two one-person bathrooms just off the dance floor. I pushed the door open to a concrete rectangle covered in graffiti and bumper stickers with a single naked light bulb hanging down. In the corner of the bathroom someone had scrawled in a thick pen, *If my dreams stood before me as years, I would live forever.*

I was peeing and thinking about how that was the most profound piece of graffiti I'd ever encountered when the door burst open. Shocked, I saw a tiny woman with pink and brown hair slam the door shut behind her. She came up behind me and slid her hands around my torso, taking my cock in her hand while running her tongue up the inside of my neck to my ear.

"This is a first," I said. She shook me as I finished. I turned around and pushed her against the wall, a hand up her shirt cupping a breast while grinding into her. She dropped to her knees and took me into her mouth, fully and completely, and then stood back up an instant later, spinning out of my grip and dashing to the door. She ripped it open and, with one backwards grin, disappeared. I got myself back together, pausing to read the graffiti once more.

If my dreams stood before me as years, I would live forever.

That touched something deep inside of me, some part of my soul I'd sensed but never felt. I went straight to the bar, ordered two shots, paid my tab, and found Carissa on the dance floor with three guys attempting to dance with her. She was watching me, though, with intense desire. As I got closer I saw a devilish grin emerge as she made eye contact with each of the three guys before turning her back to them and throwing herself onto me. All three of them looked vaguely insulted and angry, making me laugh. We downed our shots.

"Let's get the fuck out of here," Carissa said, sounding a little drunk.

"I danced!"

"You did, baby," she said, "you did!"

We tumbled out the door and into a beautiful warm spring night.

"Cartwheel!" she yelled at me, and I complied, planting my hands on the sidewalk and throwing my legs over themselves in a move I hadn't attempted in fifteen years. Carissa ran at me and jumped, and I caught her in my arms. "Take me home and fuck my brains out, writer-man," she said, so loudly that a man passing us laughed.

"Sometimes you gotta do what the lady wants," he said. We giggled and hailed a cab. Once home, we took the stairs to the apartment two at a time. I turned the three locks in quick succession, *poppoppop* and kicked the door open, pulling off my shirt even before the door had closed behind us. I ripped her clothes off and my own at the same time, and we fell onto the floor clawing and kissing and grappling each other, and when I came she wiggled her body down and took me into her mouth. She then collapsed backwards, and I fell on top of her.

"Holy fuck," she breathed into my ear, "you taste good."

I kissed her sweating neck.

"Now put me in bed."

I laughed. "You're like a dude. You cum, and you're asleep before the orgasm ends."

"Ppfft," she breathed. "Most men would kill to have a chick like me."

"That's true. That's why I love you so much."

I unfolded the bed and she fell into it and was asleep before I'd even gotten the sheets up and around her. I kissed her cheek, then sat on the edge of the bed and watched her face for a few long moments.

Outside there was the stutter of a siren. A few shouts went out before the unmistakable high-pitched crack of a gun, followed by more shouting and more sirens, and then it all faded to a different block and far enough into the background that it blended in with all the other noises of the city.

I opened the fridge and pulled out a beer, crossed the apartment to the security grate, and looked out over the fire escape before fetching an old cigarette from a coat pocket. I grabbed my notebook and a pen, pulled a towel off the rack, and stepped onto the metal balcony naked.

I spread the towel and sat. The fire escape overlooked the backs of the buildings of Fourteenth and Thirteenth streets. Nearly all the windows facing me were dark except for a few blue, busy curtains illuminated from within by the moving lights of a television.

I leaned back onto the cold brick of the building, lit the cigarette and took a sip of beer. At twenty-two I felt both young and old, like time was working against me even as a nearly infinite amount seemed at my disposal. It was a disquieting urgency wrapped in a field of spaciousness as vast as the sky, confining and liberating all at once. I took another deep pull on my cigarette, knowing I was standing at the threshold of my own adult life.

I'd finished a novel before I'd left my early twenties. Even if it was a complete piece of shit, it mattered. A badly written novel was still a novel, and if it never saw the light of day it had nevertheless transformed me. I'd come to love the odd corners of the nights, working strange shifts in dead-end jobs while living around outsiders and artists and eccentrics. And, harder to admit, I loved the ambition, the incredibly slim chance that I could be famous, take my own place in the ranks of influential writers. It seemed an outrageous thought but I allowed it to run through me, let it inspire and terrify me until, overwhelmed, I finally pushed it aside.

I took another deep drag, watching the smoke funnel out of my mouth. There was so much more locked inside me, things the novel hadn't touched, ideas and thoughts and feelings I was still trying to understand. I wanted to put all of them on paper, explore all of them as deeply as I was able.

My eyes went to the distended bellies of clouds illuminated by the city's lights, looking engorged and in need of relief. I lifted my pen and opened the notebook and started to write in drunken, pondering sentences that I would hate in the morning, but which seem profound and powerful under the first few drops of rain.

If my dreams stood before me as years, I would live forever.

I looked at that phrase, envious that I had not thought of it, and wondered who might have. Someone famous? A frustrated poet? A college student struck by a momentary flash of genius?

I leaned my head onto the brick, feeling an unbearable aliveness in me. I shivered again, turned the bottom of the beer bottle up until it was empty. I threw it into the night, smiling as I heard it smash somewhere below. I climbed back in through the open window and into bed. I pulled Carissa close, breathing in the smell of her neck, letting my thoughts drift into a future unbound by fear, as vast and limitless as dreams.

Thursday

Logan," Michael says as I'm standing in the office kitchen pouring a cup of coffee.

"Hey," I reply. Michael, the CEO, is wearing his usual outfit: skinny jeans, blue flannel shirt with the sleeves rolled to the elbow. His eyes are animated and he seems like he's over-caffeinated, focused on a new big idea, or both.

"I read that piece for HBR," he says.

I take a sip of coffee. He's talking about the *Harvard Business Review* article I wrote. It's early for me, just past nine, and my brain is only working at half speed. I nod.

"It's just, well, it's not really my voice. It doesn't sound like me."

"Well," I offer a smile. "I did write it."

"Right," he shakes his head. "Of course that makes perfect sense. But ... " He looks up to the ceiling.

"But it's not in your voice."

"Yeah."

"I get it. Do you have any writing samples?"

He leans in. "Listen: I can barely write a goddamn complete sentence. I talk. I think. I'm an idea guy, not a writer guy. That's why I have you."

"What would make it feel more like you?"

"More passionate," he replies, slapping his palm on the table. "Without being too emotional. But I'm a passionate man. I care. So just if that could come through more strongly."

"Steve did say you were passionate," I comment. "I can do passionate."

"Really? You seem quiet. Self-contained."

"Never underestimate the quiet ones."

He laughs. "Fair enough. Also the business side of the article could be a little tighter." He looks around. "In fact, meet with Jeff. He'll fill in the cracks that need to be filled." Jeff is the EVP — executive vice president — of sales.

"Okay," I say. I spot Jeff, on his cell phone, talking emphatically.

An hour later Jeff and I sit down in the worker break area outside. It's a beautiful late fall day, with a deep blue Colorado sky that makes me feel like I could just vanish into it. It's the kind of day that brings back memories of being trapped inside a school building, watching through glass as a perfect autumn afternoon went slowly to ruin.

Jeff is a short man who, like all the sales executives I've ever known, is both high in energy and extremely extroverted. He has a shaved head, large ears that stretch out away from a prominent nose, and a non-existent chin. He looks like a big inverted egg.

"Logan!" he says loudly. "Michael gave me the 4-1-1. So let's get into it, okay?" He continues talking without waiting for me to respond. "Tell me, what do you know about compliance?"

"Well," I say, "it's the stuff that used to be done by lawyers and now is mostly done by other executives; it's the work nobody wants to do but, if done right, prevents huge lawsuits."

"Close," he says, leaning in toward me, the sole object of attention honed like a predator's. "To be candid, compliance is for lawyers who couldn't handle the pressures of law firms, and for managers who can't handle the demands of making profits. It's a backwater, viewed by most companies as just that." He speaks quickly, not wasting the space between his words.

"Compliance officers usually come in after something has caught fire and try to keep the company from burning down. Compliance departments *react*. They show up after the boss has fucked his secretary or a bunch of engineers have created a software that's not only totally illegal, it's utterly unethical, or after someone does some kind of insider trading bullshit. A good compliance program would have let someone at VW whistleblow that shit, and that information would have gotten to the CEO and board, assuming they weren't in on it in the first place. And that would have meant the company could have gotten out in front of it, controlled the release of information, negotiated the fines they'd pay the government, arranged to fix what was wrong, and done all the things necessary to mitigate loss and preserve their stock price. We're talking about billions here."

"But it's not just about that anymore, right? Look, we have a software here that makes what compliance officers do a lot fucking easier — half of these fucking pricks still use goddamn Post-It notes to remind themselves of shit — and I'm not even kidding you. And we're pitching an incredibly powerful, incredibly smart software solution to an analog culture, because they have a digital problem on their hands." He pauses and takes a sip of zero-calorie, flavored water, then looks around for the first time. "Fuck," he says, "it's a nice day. I'd love to be riding in this." He's a triathlete. He takes another sip of water. "Logan, I should have asked you: does cursing bother you?" His eyes are brown and clear and intense.

"No."

"Fucking-A. Okay, so listen. All that shit I said, it's just background. The real deal is this. Companies need to be compliant not to just avoid getting sued, and not to just catch ambitious employees before they do something stupid as a result of that ambition — notice I didn't say 'bad employees'? This is important. The old model said catch the bad guys before they do bad things. The new model — our model — says identify the problematic *patterns* and *pressures* that cause good guys to do bad things. Hear the difference?"

"Of course." The meeting goes on like this, giving me enough to take a new tack for the piece I'm writing for the CEO.

As our conversation wraps up and I stand to leave, Jeff puts a hand on my arm.

"Hey, Logan. You in a relationship?"

I nod. "Engaged, in fact."

"Perfect!" He gives me a million dollar smile. "You remember when you fell in love with her?"

"What?"

"In love, cowboy. You remember?"

"I guess I haven't really thought about it."

"Well, *do*! Sales tip: you get in touch with that feeling, you can sell sand at the beach. Quality moves, but passion sells."

I laugh, since we're talking about corporate compliance. "Your wife must see you as quite the hopeless romantic."

He winks. "She loves the lifestyle I give her."

I smile politely.

I sit down at my desk. Thinking of love as a sales tool. Jesus, what a fucking asshole. Love seems so far from me these days, like remembering a long-distant vacation you had when you were a kid. You remember you had fun, but don't remember the fun feeling itself. And yet I find myself pulled into another memory even though it just seems to make everything harder and more confusing.

In the memory I'm back at a restaurant that was carved into an art deco shopping center where the ceiling was an undulating wave of concrete that came in high at the west and dipped down to a dozen or so feet high at the bar, and then ascended back to the east. Booths rimmed the edges, but we sat at a table by a window overlooking the parking lot. In the near distance the mountains erupted across the skyline, growing from green to white as they ascended. The decor was modern and minimalist.

It was not long after we'd started dating.

"So what's new?" I asked.

"I need a new website," she moaned. "The one I have now is such an embarrassment!"

"I know," I joked. "I saw it when I was busy stalking you."

She laughed. "New website, the book, and a whole new angle for my coaching. More of a female professional focus: how to build and scale a business as a female businesswoman or entrepreneur."

I nodded.

A server, a young and attractive boy who I guessed was in college, approached us with menus and a humorously self-serious manner. He held one hand across his heart as he set the menus down.

"Your menus," he intoned as if holy relics had just been placed on the table. "Specials tonight are our *asparagi bianchi* — white asparagus, English peas, prosciutto, and fennel as a starter. And black cod as an entrée, with mushrooms and dill, with burja."

"Why thank you, kind sir," I responded, making her smile over her menu at me. Her small diamond earrings split the restaurant's lights into little red, yellow, and blue fractals, as did the small diamond hanging from her neck.

"I can help you with the web stuff," I offered when the waiter left.

"I would really appreciate that." She reached out and touched my hand.

"Sure. So how's the book?"

"I don't know how you write them," she laughed. "It's not easy."

"I don't know how I do it either. It might have been beginner's luck for me."

"I read your novel."

"Oh?" I felt my breath hitch and pretended to keep reading the menu.

"It's really good," she said. "I can't believe you wrote that when you were so young. It's good — it's really good," she repeated. "I mean, it's dark! But it's so ... intimate. Like I was with those characters. I really enjoyed it." A pause. "It's really good," she repeated.

"Oh, I know," I said in mock earnestness. "Talent is my burden to bear in this life."

But she didn't take the bait. "I've noticed," she said, "that you make a joke whenever I try to compliment you."

I laughed uneasily. "It usually works."

She considers that as our waiter appears.

"And have we made any decisions? Perhaps some beverages to start us out? Wine, perhaps?"

I looked over to her. "Waiters do the trick when my dodging doesn't work." She smiled. "Wine?"

"Sure. But only one glass for me."

"I'll drink the rest," I said, half kidding. I opened the wine list and scanned. "Four Rivers Pinotage."

"Yes sir." He departed with a bow.

I let out a little sigh. "I'll try not to deflect so much," I said. "Old habits."

"That book came out — what — ten years ago?"

"Something like that."

"What was the second book you didn't like?"

"I tried to write the Great American Novel as a follow-up, something serious and literary and chock full of references to other great works; more *Paris Review* and less Barnes and Noble."

"The one you self-published."

I nodded.

"Cost you a lot."

I nodded again.

She considered thoughtfully. "Why didn't you just do print on demand?"

"Didn't exist back then. Neither did Amazon — or at least not like it exists now."

"Oh. And now?"

"Now," I said, "I have a fantastic idea, and it's going well."

"Can you tell me?"

I laughed. "Not yet. I haven't worked out how to talk about it yet without taking up all of dinner."

She shrugged and looked around.

"I want to get it down to a coffee-sized conversation first."

A laugh. "Okay."

"The trouble is I have to work my freelance gigs, and it's tough to chase down money, do writing work for clients, and then write for myself. I've been working on this for like two years now, and can't lock in a big chunk of time to get it right."

She nodded. "I can appreciate that. I was in Spain for most of my twenties. I needed to get away from ... all of it. Family, the States, the whole thing. Was a great time, but it was a pain in the ass with the work visas and all. Trying to live the life we want to live and make a decent living isn't so easy."

"Sounds like it was really amazing. I'm a little jealous. Do you miss traveling?"

"If I don't travel out of the country at least once a year, I'll lose my mind," she laughed. "I don't have the travel bug; it's survival for me. You?"

"Not that much. My writing and my lifestyle are all designed for minimum financial burn, and travel is expensive. But I do want to do more of it, when time and circumstances allow." I took a sip of water. "I need a wealthy wife."

"I wish you luck in finding one!" She reached out and touched my hand again, this time more slowly, running her finger from my wrist across to my thumb. The waiter returned for the pouring and tasting routine, then departed with our food orders.

"Okay," I said, taking a big swallow of wine. "Here's the thing: in order to finish this book the way it needs to be written, I need freedom.

ONLY EVERYTHING

Time. A clear head. Space. The only way I know how to do that is to have financial freedom." I paused and looked out the window of the restaurant, my eyes lingering on the mountains. I spoke again while looking at them. "I could divest my savings. Retirement. All the money I've squirrelled away over the years. It's not much. Fifty, maybe sixty K. Enough to live for eighteen or so months if I watch myself. But once that's done, I'm broke and pushing forty years old. Risky."

She considered. "Is it the only way you'll write the book you know you can write?"

"I think so. I think this one is so much better than the first. I think it can be a best seller, maybe a movie, but I've got to go all in to do it. I can't be a part time artist."

She nodded solemnly.

"What do you think?"

"I think you should go for it," she said without moment's hesitation. "I read that first book. It's brilliant. I think you need to take the leap."

By the time our entrees had arrived, I realized something that was even more surprising than my decision to put all my life savings into writing a book: I was falling in love. We went back to my apartment after dinner and made love for the first time. I had never felt so connected to another human being. Afterwards, in the low light of the room, I lay next to her looking at the light across her full breasts and exposed belly.

"I love you," I said, quietly. Although she didn't respond, she did smile and turn to me. It would take another week before she said those words back to me, and by then it seemed like our lives were bound for something greater, brighter, happier than either of us had managed on our own.

I look up from my computer, back in the open space office of Trudent. I don't feel much inspired to write about what I'm being paid to write about, but I do my best. By four o'clock I've finished the piece and emailed it off to Michael, Steve, and Jeff. I go out to clear my head. To the right of the employee outside lounge is an alleyway that is lower than the lounge by ten feet. There I can see the heads of Steve and Michael.

" ... on the floor. That fucking thing ... right? Tell me I'm *wrong!*" Michael is speaking in barely under a shout, and although I have no idea what he's talking about it's obvious he's furious about something.

Steve is facing me and is easiest to hear.

"Yes. It's a mess now, but we'll take care of it. We've been understaffed — not an excuse — but I've got the right team in place now. We're going to cover the gap. The figures from this week — "

Michael says something I can't make out and appears to jab Steve in the chest with a finger.

"I get it," Steve says. "I'll get on a plane tonight. Tonight, okay? I'll be there by eight, and we'll get it all figured out. These things happen ... "

"These things do not just happen!" Michael explodes. "They happen because people like you *fuck up!* Now get your fucking team together or get yourself another fucking job! Am I clear?"

"Yes. I'll take care of it."

Michael turns back toward the offices by a set of stairs leading to a metal door. I watch him moving intensely through the office; people clear a path as he storms past them.

A few moments later Steve comes up the side stairs to the employee pit. His head is down and his face flushed. His hair is, of course, in its perfect blonde wave.

"Hey man," I say as he passes me passes me, startling him.

"Oh, hey!"

"You okay?"

"What?"

"That looked kind of intense."

"That?" He looks over his shoulder. "Oh, no. No, that's fine. Michael is just passionate. He just really cares."

"Really cares?"

A nod.

I smile a little. "My dad cared too. Had to do a few years of therapy to undo that kind of care."

Steve's blue eyes stare blankly back for a moment. Then he offers one of his cherub smiles.

"TMI, Logan," he says, a little laugh for punctuation so that I know he's not too serious. "That kind of sharing makes me uncomfortable." He laughs a little more. "It's all good, right? It's my responsibility to make sure we're all set up and, as you know — we had a rocky start to this quarter with all the missing team members — and I should have just thought that one through when I made my last board presentation? It's all good." He pauses. "Really. Thanks for asking."

I nod. "Okay."

Spring, 1996

Alejandro leaned back on his white leather couch, collared shirt unbuttoned almost to the navel, facing double doors of glass and white curtains that opened onto a spacious deck where Franklin and I perched. The light overhead caught Alejandro's pants, fine black leather, and threw a pool of shadow across them. In his right hand was the printout, in the left a martini. A cigarette burned from a nearby ashtray. His reading glasses were a stylish bright red frame and, with his legs crossed, he looked like he could be the director of an art house movie.

He had been in this apartment since the late eighties and the rent control meant he was paying about a third of what the market would normally get for a one-bedroom with a tenth-story balcony looking south.

Franklin, Alejandro, and I had eaten a Mediterranean-themed dinner at Alejandro's place, and afterwards Alejandro had asked for some time alone to gather his thoughts about my manuscript, which he had read already. This was where we left him — with the martini, the reading glasses, the manuscript, and the burning cigarette.

Franklin and I stood on the spacious deck, looking out over the city.

"The book is really good, man.."

It was a warm spring evening and the air of Manhattan had just enough moisture in it to remind me of the ocean. We looked across the city.

"Thanks, but you're not exactly a literary critic."

"Indeed." He tilted his head toward the door. "That one, though — he reads four novels a month. He's a machine. And he tells it like it is."

"I know," I said, swallowing some of my drink.

"You'll be okay. He likes you. If he doesn't like the book he'll be gentle." Franklin glanced in at Alejandro. "Probably."

I laughed. "This is just my first go at it. You've been at it for almost a decade already. You ever think about giving up?"

Franklin leaned out over the railing, his blue eyes far away. He took another sip and looked down Broadway for so long I wasn't sure he'd heard me. Just as I was about to repeat myself, he spoke.

"In low moments. Yeah. Which sometimes come a few times in a day." A humorless laugh. "I think about not just giving up but burning everything I've ever created." His handsome profile narrowed, hardening around the eyes. "But I'm not ready to hang it up. The teaching gig only takes up a dozen hours a week — but of course the pay isn't enough to live on."

He took another sip. I looked from his profile back to the city, to the lights far below reflecting off the shining rooftops of passing cars.

"If you spend most of your days punching a clock, you're a clock-puncher no matter what you do in your free time," he said, his voice soft and barely audible above the ambient noise of New York. "But the odds of success?" He shook his head. "Alejandro is older than me by fifteen years; older than you by a generation. He's been trying to break into this thing since he was your age."

"And he hasn't given up."

"Not yet. But it takes its toll." He still talked with his profile to me.

"How far do you want to take it?"

"What?" He turned for a moment.

"Your art. How far."

He looked away. "All the way," he said.

I looked back to the city. An ambulance turned onto Broadway, lights on but sirens off. It flew away from us in a silent urgency, the absence of sound making it eerily beautiful.

"Household name," Franklin said, not much louder than a whisper. "Museums. Galleries. Art books."

I glanced over but he was focused in the distance.

"Holy shit."

He shrugged. "Why else play the game if not to win?"

I had no answer for that.

"What about you, Logan?" He turned to me.

"What about me?"

"What motivates you?"

"I dunno," I admitted. "I mean, I'd love to make a living writing books. How great would that be? But I'm just a nobody writing a silly little novel about life."

"Isn't that what Hemingway did?"

I laughed. "No. He wrote about the things that drive life. Love. Longing. War. Desire. Determination. Death. Writing was just the bones he hung his ideas off. I just wanna write a decent book."

Franklin shook his head. "Seems like that's what he did." He took a drink. "How are you judging yourself if not against the greats?"

It was my turn to shrug.

"It's a lot of work, writing a novel," he observed.

I looked back to the ambulance, now twenty blocks away and fading fast. I wondered about the lives inside.

"Darlings," a voice rang out. Franklin and I turned. Alejandro hadn't moved except to put the manuscript down.

"Moment of truth," Franklin said.

I walked back inside and helped myself to one of Alejandro's smokes.

"Logan," Alejandro said, serene and serious. "Sit down."

I sat and grabbed an ashtray.

"Two smokes inside of a month. That's it. Usually mine and whoever I'm fucking. Otherwise the place smells like a VFW club. So that's your first and last inside."

I nodded.

"Very, very good," he stated. "You should be proud of yourself."

I didn't move at all, almost like I was waiting for a slap to come.

"You've captured something only someone much older and much more experienced should know."

I took a deep drag on the cigarette and looked at my shoes, wingtip black hand-me-downs from Franklin. They were getting scratched and worn, I noticed.

"Logan."

I looked up. Alejandro was regal in the chair with his shockingly full black hair standing over a set and serious face.

"The book is good, very good. I won't lie to you; I like you too much. It's not perfect, and some parts betray a lack of life experience. But you're only in your early twenties and it has moments of intense clarity and pockets of genuine brilliance, and it's better than about half of the books I've read in my life. That sounds like a backhanded compliment, but I want you to consider your age and that this is your first book. So I have one suggestion for you: send it in. They'll help you polish it."

I took another drag and looked out at my brother's silhouette. "You really think a major publisher would be interested?"

He uncrossed his legs and sat forward, elbows on his knees. "I'm just telling you it's good enough to send in."

I nodded, holding onto each one of the negative words as I'd heard them. *Inexperienced. Not as good as half of the books he'd read. Pockets of brilliance.*

"Is there anything else you need from me?"

"I'd love to know where you don't think it's good enough."

He shook his head. "Don't peddle your insecurities to me, Logan. I said it was good. Now don't go and fuck that up by getting all neurotic on me and focusing on the negative. Send it in."

Reluctantly I nodded. "Okay. But say a little more, please."

He sighed. "God knows I'm no editor." He paused. "The places it's not as strong are the places you'll need to live more years to get right." He smiled, but an ache of sadness came through his brown eyes. When he spoke again I could hear the strain of emotion in his voice. "I wish you wouldn't have to experience the things life still needs to show you, but you can't be an artist if you don't suffer and admit to your suffering. You're becoming a novelist, and a novelist writes about the present by giving voice to the past, to all the pain he's tried to leave there. There's pain here," he tapped the printout. "Longing, heartache. But the pain goes deeper than you can yet imagine."

We sat in silence. Franklin's back was to us on the deck outside.

"That," he said at last, "is the only thing missing, but you haven't lived enough years to fill that in. Send it in. Trust me."

I nodded and looked up. "Okay. Thank you."

"Of course. If we don't help each other, what's the point? We seem all alone in the universe, Logan, except that we have each other. And that's comforting. Now, I think I'm ready for a change of scenery, yes?"

"Sure." I felt a surge of pride and shame at being both better than I thought and not as good as I wanted to be.

"Franklin!"

My brother's silhouette turned.

"What are you doing?"

"Waiting for you two."

"Well, baby needs a cocktail. Dinner and art hour are over." He smiled at me and stood up. "It's time we go out," he licked his lips and winked, "and spread our scent."

Summer, 1996

Carissa slept soundly as usual. When she slept she was immobile, almost like she'd been drugged. I could move all around her, spoon her, get out of bed, and almost nothing would cause her to do much more than stir. I was envious, as for me sleep was often a challenge. I had been tossing and turning for an hour, maybe more, getting close to sleep but watching it dart away whenever it was nearly in my grasp. Defeated, I finally rose and put my feet onto the cold wood and yawned. I pulled on jeans.

I poured a little wine into a glass and contorted my way onto the fire escape without spilling a drop. It was overcast and quiet. Now early summer, there was no real difference between the outside and inside temperature. My mind was like a spooked mule tied to a pole, cutting patterns of worry into the same circular groove, round and round and round. The wine didn't help, and when it began drizzling I didn't move even as I started to shiver.

A hand touched my shoulder and I nearly screamed.

Carissa leaned halfway out the window.

"Sorry," she said sleepily, a small hand covering her yawn.

"*Jesus*," I breathed. "I almost leapt off!"

"Sorry," she repeated. "What are you doing up, baby? Can't sleep?"

I shook my head.

"How long have you been sitting here?"

"Not long." I didn't really know. Everything was moving at the wrong speed, tinged with fear and exhaustion and a sense of unreality.

"Is everything okay?"

"No," I admitted. "I'm going to run out of money again. I don't know what I'm doing. And I don't think I can write."

"Ah," she said, "*that* kind of insomnia. Let's go get a drink."

I looked at her without understanding, the mule beginning to drag fatalistic thoughts through their rut again. "What?"

But she was already back inside. She tossed the comforter to the floor, momentarily exposing her naked body. A light blinked on and I saw her grabbing overalls and a light sweater.

"Come," she called. "Get your shoes."

"What?" I was confused.

"You, baby. Me. Let's go get some beers."

"But you have to work tomorrow."

"I'll be fine. No discussion. Get dressed."

"Carissa — "

"Now, Logan!"

I slid inside and pulled on a hoodie and hooked a pair of flip flops with my toes. She was already at the door, purse slung across her shoulder and hair a tangled mess of colors.

"Ready?"

"Are you sure?" I was still in the fog of insomnia, half expecting to wake up next to her. "Come on," she smiled.

We went down the stairs and into the drizzle of a Tuesday night. Most of East Village's bars closed earlier on weekdays but a few of the more hardcore places would serve until the four o'clock last call. That gave us plenty of time, and a heavy metal bar close to our house was still open. We went inside, happy not to be met by a wall of smoke and leather and piercing music. Instead it was mostly empty, with a neck-tattooed man behind the bar who offered us a grunt. His hair was dyed an impossible shade of black.

Carissa pulled out two bars stools, directing me into one. I sat. Everything felt surreal. What I wanted was to be asleep.

"Double whiskey for him," she said. "Something decent."

"Red Label?"

"Sure. I'll take a vodka tonic. Well is fine." The drinks were in front of us a moment later, without a word. She set a twenty on the bar.

I exhaled, looking ahead at a mirror, the black bar, and the black ceiling and floor. Thrash metal that descended from the corners of the room at a surprisingly reasonable volume. The big double whiskey looked good and went down fast. I nodded for another.

"You'd be crazy if you weren't nervous," Carissa said. "I'd have trouble sleeping too."

"You'd never have trouble sleeping."

She smiled sideways at me. The pinks of her hair had been replaced with greens. "Well, that's true. But maybe I wouldn't sleep *as* deeply."

I laughed. "It's just — that manuscript is sitting with motherfucking Random House *right now*. I'm sure they hate it. I'm sure they're going to reject it tomorrow. I'm sure I embarrassed Rebecca by even sending it in. I'm sure they think I'm really fifteen, not twenty-two."

"Uh huh," she said, "I'm *sure* that's exactly what's a happening. Since you're so sure, why can't you sleep?"

I smiled. "Yeah, I know I'm being ridiculous. Nothing new there." I put my hand on her leg. "Tell me about your day." I didn't want to talk about myself.

"I already did," she said. "It was nothing very exciting. You — "

"You told me that your boss," I interrupted, "flipped his wig today."

"Yeah," she said, laughing. "What an asshole."

"But he does have the world's greatest assistant office manager."

"Oh stop. I'm an overpaid secretary."

"Don't sell yourself short, baby. One day you could be *the* office manager."

"I hadn't thought about that," she replied, looking wistfully at the ceiling. "One day I could be making coffee for the *boss* instead of the boss's *assistant*. You know, I'm so lucky to have you to help me aim high."

"Well, here's to unlimited ambition." We clinked classes and laughed.

"You know," she said, sipping her drink. "First off, you should smoke a cigarette."

"You should really just start buying your own packs."

"I don't smoke!"

"Yeah yeah."

I lit one and passed it to her. We sat for a moment in the blacked-out, thrash metal bar, with the maladjusted bartender glaring at the wall.

"I know I'm kind of drifting here," she said, glancing at me.

That caught me off guard. "Drifting?"

"In life. You're sweet to never say anything."

I considered. "I dunno. I mean, I love you no matter what you do. Plus you're not so insane as to work a catering job while putting all your eggs into an artist's flimsy basket."

For a moment she looked younger than her twenty-two years. "For now it's enough for me to just work at Rockefeller Center, and be with you, and live in this crazy city." She looked at me. "I don't have any idea what I want to do as an adult."

"I'm learning," I said, "that most adults don't know either. It's weird. I guess we are adults."

"I sure don't feel like one."

"My god. Me either."

"I guess I sometimes feel self-conscious," she admitted. "You and your brother are so ambitious."

I laughed. "I don't know what we are. Both full of shit, perhaps."

She raised an eyebrow. "I'm not done."

"I accepted a compliment prematurely."

"Well," she said, "I also see how hard it can be. I see it with you, like tonight. And I see it with your brother."

I took a sip of my second drink.

"How in Franklin?" He seemed impossibly confident to me.

"Well, his eyes. Underneath those shiny blues and that smile there's a lot going on. A *lot*. I don't think I'd want to live behind those eyes."

"Huh."

"Too much?"

"No; I think you're right. It's just interesting. Never thought about it like that. Sometimes I wish I could be more like you, you know? Just work a job and enjoy life. It's an easier way to do things."

"Yeah," she said, putting a foot up on the side of the bar. "But you can."

"Right. No victims here."

"And you *say* that, but you don't mean it. Rocky. You're in this for the *fight*, admit it. I'm here for the *show*."

I laughed.

"So entertain me, *bitch*!"

I laughed again.

"How did Paul Simon song go? 'He cried out in his anger and his shame, I am leaving I am leaving but the fighter still remains.' That's you, darling."

"You know," I said with a shake of my head, "I think I want to talk about something that's actually going to make me tired."

She smiled. "I talked to my mother this morning."

"Oh boy." I feigned a yawn.

"Oh boy is right. So Marcie got into a huge fight with Dan. About the wedding. Again. She ended up sleeping on my mom's couch."

I laughed. "Your fucking family. What an insane asylum."

She rolled her eyes. "That's not the half of it. Marcie got drunk first, so she woke my mom up because she was so bombed she was snoring like a lumberjack; and then my mom couldn't wake her up. Almost called the paramedics."

It felt good to hear her talk, and as the drinks went down and the night deepened, I felt something shift and lighten inside me. An hour later we walked home in the deep belly of the morning, fingers intertwined, the rain now a gentle mist under the yellowed light of street lamps. The city was so quiet it was as if there were only two of us in all of New York, and when we got back to the apartment I easily found sleep, with Carissa pulled tightly against me.

Summer, 1996

Oh, give me a break," Alejandro scoffed. "That fucking queen needs to step it back a notch." He was wearing a white suit that was utterly out of place in New York City.

"He was insistent. If I go with their gallery, no other reps and I have to give them a cut of any work sold outside of the gallery."

"Oh, I knew *Robert*," Alejandro snapped, "when he was still *Bob* from *Poughkeepsie*. He was a hack with no talent who wisely decided he should get into selling art instead of making it."

Franklin shrugged. "He was firm."

"Ask Princess Nosehair whatever happened to Xavier," Alejandro said. "Bob's lover back in the day, and his first big break as an art dealer, who Bob ruined by overinflating the poor, talentless boy's head with ideas of grandeur, when the truth was if he'd had an original thought it would have died of loneliness."

"Jesus," Jackson laughed.

We were sitting around a semi-circular table in the back of a bar in Midtown. It was one of the interchangeable plastic paddys of the city, the formulaic Irish pubs. This one was a long rectangle of a space with the bar on the left and seating on the right. It had all the token Irish bar clichés: the flags, the antique signs from the Second World War, framed pictures of Irish soccer teams no one had heard of. We had ducked in there to get out of a rain storm, and I'd had to call Carissa from a pay phone, in a downpour, to let her know where to meet us. Franklin sat next to me, Jackson was next to him, and then Alejandro. The whole place was overrun with the stale and starchy smell of fryer grease with an undercurrent of days-old beer.

"You know, they should have red and white checkered tablecloths to complete the look," Alejandro noted.

"At least they know how to pour a drink," Jackson said. "This gin and tonic is about ninety-five percent gin." Although Jackson was always studiously thorough in removing any grease from his hands and arms, he had missed a smudge on his right ear. He turned to Franklin. "You're telling me," he said, his smile exaggerated, "that this guy wants a cut of every painting you sell, no matter if he has a hand in selling it or not? That if you sell something to me, right here and now, a fucking cocktail napkin with a sketch on it for ten bucks, he gets a cut?"

Franklin nodded. "A lot of the preeminent galleries do that now."

Jackson laughed. "I'm with Alejandro on this one. Sounds like a racket."

"It is," Franklin agreed, "and that racket is called the art world." He was introspective and serious; he had told me beforehand the gallery was a major deal and, if he took it, there could be a big pick up in his work, but he was such a ruthlessly ambitious self-promoter and seller that Bob from Poughkeepsie would be getting one hell of a deal and might, in fact, be getting in Franklin's way.

"The business is so corrupt," Alejandro sighed, taking a sip of his drink. "I mean, I guess it's been that way for a long time. Fucking Warhol was a criminal."

"And a genius," Franklin said quietly.

"A criminal," Alejandro said. "But still. Princess Nosehair has done a good job of making connections. Could be a real lift for you, but it would be like working with your balls in a vice."

The door to the bar opened up and Carissa stepped through, dripping with rain. She closed her umbrella before spotting us.

"Gimme a shot," she said to the bartender on her way in. "Stat. Vodka. Well."

He poured it and she downed it at the bar. "Plus a black and tan." She came the rest of the way to us.

"Hey babe," I stood and kissed her. "You're wet!"

"It *is* raining," she said.

"Hey doll," Jackson stood and kissed her cheek. "Been awhile."

"Yeah, I see these other alcoholics a lot more often."

As she hugged Alejandro and Franklin and sat down, I noticed that she was very pale and her eyes wide. When she reached to get her beer from the bartender there was a shake to her hands.

"You okay?" I asked.

She gave a false laugh. "Just some subway drama."

"Oh?"

"Do tell," Alejandro said.

"Nice suit," she said.

"Thanks."

"Tom Wolfe called. He wants his cliché back," Jackson said.

"No sweetie; my cane and tap shoes are in the car out front," Alejandro replied.

"Well, I was getting onto the train. Rush hour, you know?"

"Packed," Jackson agreed, nodding. "Nightmare."

"Yeah. So we're at Thirty-third and this guy starts yelling, like really yelling, right before the train comes to a stop. He's talking about, I don't even know what. Government, white people, the UN, just crazy shit, and I'm only maybe ten people from him, and then he pulls out a knife, like a big goddamn knife and everyone screams and there's a big push and he slashes and it hits some businessman in the arm but it would have been his face if the guy hadn't been faster and that guy like yells and falls back and he's like bleeding and everyone is scrambling and pushing and screaming and then the doors open up — "

"The doors open — like the train came to a stop?"

"Yeah, at Thirty-third, and the guy with the knife is standing with his back to the doors. Some black dude kicks him in the chest and he goes flying out the door and then out of one of the other cars — the one right next to us — a guy comes running and he's got a gun out. 'NYPD' he shouts and screams for the dude to get on his knees."

The whole table had gone quiet. Van Morrison's *Brown Eyed Girl* played in the background.

"Holy shit," Jackson said finally.

"Right? I had to get out at the next stop and then ride back up."

"What happened to the guy with the knife?" Franklin asked.

"I don't know — it looked like the undercover cop was on top of it."

"Train kept moving?" Alejandro asked. "No one hit the emergency stop?"

"Don't think so."

"People didn't want to be inconvenienced anymore," Jackson said.

"Or it didn't work," Franklin noted.

"Oh honey, I'm sorry. What about the businessman?"

"It looked like a nurse or doctor was on our train and helping him when I got off. But I don't know. There was blood everywhere. People were slipping on it."

"That's fucked up," Jackson said. "I saw a guy get stabbed once, in Queens, F train at Parsons. Stabbed in the back and the dude ran off. Think he killed him. Fucking bled all over the fucking place."

"My roommate in college got his front teeth knocked out in a robbery," Franklin commented. "They tried to kill him but he was able to get away."

"Nurse!" Alejandro called, "Shots please. Vodka. Top shelf. Your choice — five of 'em." He looked around the table. "I was robbed at gun point in the late eighties. Times Square. Stole my wallet and my watch and pistol-whipped me."

We did our shots as the rain let up.

"Let's get the fuck out of this Irish stank hole," Alejandro said. "If I have to smell a fryer for one more second I'm going to vomit."

"I need to go home and get a bath," Carissa said.

Franklin nodded, and Jackson hugged her. "You should go with her," he said to me. "We'll see you guys the next time."

"Can we walk?" she asked.

"Sure, baby."

I tossed a twenty on the table. "Have fun."

I took the umbrella, but it was no longer raining. We started walking south, holding hands, moving so slowly that we were getting passed on both sides by New Yorkers rushing home.

"I'm kind of freaked, you know?"

"I bet. I would be too."

But she shook her head. "I always felt safe here, even though of course it's *not* safe, not ever. But tonight I felt how close we all are to each other here, and how many fucked-up and dangerous people live in this city. I mean, that businessman would be dead if he hadn't gotten an arm up. It can be all over for you in a flash here." She looked at me with those big green eyes. "I felt, I felt — I felt my blood go cold, like it could be me. Like it was a warning."

"Let's get you a bath and get you warmed up. Maybe take a cab to work next week, just until it doesn't seem so intense?"

She nodded, lowering her head as she walked, and I could see her lower lip trembling. I put my arm around her.

"Crazy — *real* crazy — is about as scary a thing as there is," I said. "I mean, we talk about crazy friends and exes and shit, but when we encounter someone who is really fucking *mad*, and really fucking *dangerous*, that's some scary shit."

"You're telling me."

"How about I make dinner tonight?"

"I'm not hungry."

"That's okay. You can just move it around your plate."

She smiled a little and I held her closer.

"I love you," I said. "I won't let anyone hurt you." It was a stupid thing to say and an empty promise, but she leaned hard into me anyway and I felt her soften under my arm.

"Oh, Logan," she breathed, "just take me home and fuck me."

Thursday Night

Usual?" Griffin asks.

I nod.

"We have a nice bourbon from Wyoming, brewed in micro batches," he says, pushing his oversized glasses up a nose that looks too small to hold them. "They actually managed to get their hands on a bunch of old wine barrels that they aged cabernet in for fifty years." He waits for the appropriate level of impact.

"No shit?"

"No shit," he replies with a touch of satisfaction. Griffin is a twenty-something with brown hair pushed into a side part, his face slight and boyishly handsome. He's dressed in a gray shirt with the sleeves rolled neatly to the elbow, while his Dijon-colored tie features blue stars erupting in its fabric. A tweed vest hangs off his shoulders and his blue jeans are rolled up to show red socks.

His knowledge of libations seems limitless; he can pontificate not only on the finer points of any spirit in the house but also on the history of that particular spirit, where and when it was created, and how it has evolved over centuries. Here he is the unchallenged master of the space and runs his bar with a combination of perfectionism and playfulness.

"Here." He pours a small taste. I smell it and take a sip. It's full on the tongue with a hint of tannins and oak on the back end.

"Fantastic," I say.

He nods and pours me a glass. "Lion's Stout as well?"

"Sure."

The bar is an English-styled pub, but it's entirely top-shelf, local and organic, and artisan. It's a small square room with an antique piano near the door, benches with animal furs thrown across them on two walls, a hardwood floor, and a bar on the right as you come in, featuring converted industrial equipment next to items that look like they were bought directly from an English estate. To my right a porcelain dog, white with a red collar, stares sadly off into the distance. It looks like the head comes off, presumably so some British grandmother could store her sweeties inside.

The stout is poured and the empty bottle and full glass placed on the bar in front of me.

"Are we hungry this evening?"

"Yeah," I say. "Let me have the grilled cheese with bacon."

"It's not on the menu anymore," Griffin says, "but I think we can make that happen for you. Jim," he calls, and the cook, about the same age as the Griffin, peeks out from the kitchen, a tiny four-by-six-foot space attached to the street side of the bar.

"Yeah," the man says, stepping into view. He has a greased mustache that stands an inch away from his cheeks on either side. It's a perfectly absurd look that makes me feel the chasm of age between them and me.

"You got what you need for grilled cheese with bacon?"

"Sure do."

"Gimme one?"

"Comin' right up."

A few minutes later the grilled cheese is in front of me. As I take a bite of the sandwich, the cook leans out.

"That okay?" he asks.

"Awesome," I say. "Great job."

This place is one of my sanctuaries. I'm too old to go out drinking the way I did in my younger days. And at home I'm the only one awake past nine and I can read only so many books. We're supposed to be making the transition to married life and kids and all that, but something about the early nights reminds me of all the worst parts of my youth.

Half an hour later the bar is filling up, and a dark-skinned man with gray stubble takes a seat next to me. He orders a scotch and notices my whiskey.

"Whatcha drinking?" He has a British accent tinged with the rounded edges of the working class.

I tell him.

"Sounds good. Gimme what he's having," he says to Griffin. The man is probably a decade older than me. His hair is cut close to the head, black on top and graying at the sides.

"You're out on a Thursday night," he says. "I'm guessing you don't work in an office."

I laugh. "I do, actually. But it's the first time in a long while."

"First time you're out on a Thursday in a long while?" He smiles sarcastically.

Griffin grins behind the bar but doesn't look up or say anything.

"My savings account and my liver wish that were the case," I reply, "but no. First time I've had a full-time job in awhile. Years, in fact."

"No shit. Well mate, you had a good run at it, then."

We both look off to the back end of the bar.

"You?" I ask.

"Me? Oh." He waits until his whisky is poured. "Me. How much do you want to know?"

"Whatever you feel like sharing."

He takes a sip from his drink. "Used to live in Connecticut, in a big fucking house, five thousand square feet. Worked for IBM as an IT consultant. My wife and I emigrated here in the eighties; I found a great job, and we raised two beautiful daughters."

"From India?"

"Yup."

"Nice."

He shakes his head. "No, it kinda sucked, actually. I did what I thought you're supposed to do in America. Make money. Have a big fucking house. Nice cars. Expensive private schools for the girls. My paychecks, which were huge, vanished every month inside of my even more massive expenses."

He looks at me for the first time.

"So what changed?"

"The wife passed," he says, matter-of-factly. "Cancer."

"Oh Christ. I'm sorry," I say, but he ignores my platitudinous expression of sympathy.

"With her gone, I realized I couldn't do it anymore. Didn't want to live in this shadow of a life of status and money and shit I don't need. So I talked to the girls, and I asked them if they want to pack up with their crazy old man and start over."

"They said yes?"

He laughs. "Surprisingly, they did. One was sixteen, the other was eighteen. But they were as sick of Connecticut as I was, so we moved."

"Not a lot of brown people in Connecticut."

"Fuck, mate, not a lot of brown people here, either."

I laughed. "That's true."

"But it's better here. More open spaces. Better people. Less rat race. Open minds and open hearts. So anyway, fours years now. They're both in school, and we all live in a tiny apartment. I do contract work still for IBM, which I'll keep doing till they get out of school, and then I'm going to do something else."

"Really? What?"

He takes another sip. "Fuck if I know. I tell my girls their old man's going to be doing something crazy, though. Maybe travel the world. Maybe start a business. Maybe live out of his car. But I've given enough of my life to working for a company."

A short man with a white moustache and potbelly under his apron comes up from the back of the pub, struggling with a plastic bin full of clean dishes, and goes into the kitchen. He has to be at least in his mid-fifties. The staff ignores him, with Griffin stepping aside as they talk between themselves. I wonder at what kinds of bad life events, or bad life decisions, or both, had to have happened for this man to be bussing dishes in a decade when many are putting the finishing touches on their retirement plans. I feel a swell of sadness as I see some of myself in him.

"We're on the same path, with the opposite starting point," I say at last. "I lived my whole life free of any full time job."

"And now?"

"Work full time. Fucking hate it."

"Of course you do. I can tell by looking at you you're not one for an office. So why do it?"

"I'm engaged. In a lot of debt. Thought I wanted to get married and start a family, and it seemed like the responsible thing to do."

"Now you're not so sure."

"Now I'm not so sure," I repeat. "Would you have done it differently, if you could?"

"Fuck. Who knows? All those decisions got me here, so who's to say? But if you're asking me if I'd suggest someone else take my path, I guess I'd say no."

"Why?"

"Too many years in an office making money and nothing else. I'd rather be poor and have been there for my girls, even if they went to shit public schools instead of fancy private ones. But I was too busy to be much of a father to them. Too busy to enjoy life. Too busy for my wife. Too busy to even consider what I wanted. But I woke up in time; I'm fucking grateful for that."

We sit in silence, and I drink some of my beer and finish my grilled cheese. The graying busboy emerges from the kitchen, having loaded the clean dishes into their racks. Griffin has a leg up and is still talking and joking. As the man walks by, I see Griffin's right hand slip under the bar.

"Hey," he says, glancing sideways to the man, who stops with a look like he's about to be told to do something else. A can of beer is in Griffin's hand.

"You looked thirsty."

The man's face lights up. "Oh! Thank you!" Griffin slips it into the empty bus bin and, ever the king of the understatement, goes back to his conversation as if nothing happened. Had I not been looking directly at him I would have missed the entire exchange. I smile. There's a reason this is my favorite pub.

"You love her?" the man next to me asks.

I don't have to ask who. "Of course."

"Sometimes," he says, "love requires we do something we wouldn't do if we were by ourselves."

I nod.

"Can I give you some free advice?"

"Sure."

"The thing is, when it's love – when it's really love -- it never *feels* like a sacrifice. It never *feels* like compromise. It never *feels* like you have to make some shit choice. It's just fucking beautiful, and fucking easy. And I don't know much, believe me, but if your beloved *is* your beloved, she would never allow you to sell your soul for her sake, or the sake of your family-to-be — not if that's what it felt like to you. When you really love someone you can't let them throw their life away for your own. You just can't."

My glasses are empty and my sandwich is gone. I have nothing to say to him.

"How about another round?" Griffin asks, looking over his glasses.

"No," I say with a shake of the head. "I've gotta get up for work tomorrow." I shrug. "Just the check." I offer my hand to the man next to me. "Logan."

He takes it in a firm grasp. "Ashvin. My friends call me Ash."

"I'm glad I ran into you, Ash. It's been a helpful coincidence."

"In my experience," Ash says, "there are no such things as coincidences. But believe what you will."

I pay Griffin, who offers me a handshake as well.

"See you soon, buddy," he says. I'm sure he's overheard at least some of the conversation, and his smile pulls into the tightened look of empathy.

I stand outside the pub. It's getting closer to winter. The night is brisk and dry with stars like points of fire overhead. It would be easy to blame her, I realize, to make her responsible for where I am now. But it's not that simple.

Summer, 1996

The rattle of the air conditioner mostly drowned out horns whose impatience indicated that, somewhere on the island of Manhattan, a light had turned green. Cold air streamed across our pullout bed, where I was ensconced beneath the covers away from the artificial chill. I opened an eye to see sunlight stabbing into a corner of the room, its boldness telling me I'd overslept. With a groan I sat up. The bed was folded in two quick motions, sheets and all. I plodded over to the coffee pot and hit the brew button. Carissa always set it up before she left for work, reason ten-thousand-and-one that I loved her. I poured the first cup, added milk and sugar, and then sat down at the table to rub my face and get my circuits running. By the time I had drunk the second cup, I was feeling good enough to put on my cheap sunglasses and head out the door to get a little something to eat.

The sidewalk greeted me like a slap. It was full summer, and heat seemed to be emanating from every conceivable surface: car hoods, exhaust, sidewalks, glass, and the air itself. It was humid in a way that made me imagine being inside an armpit, maybe because it smelled so much like the East Village — diesel soot, body odor, cheap perfume, animal and human piss, and trash.

I stuck close to the buildings where there was some shade, heading to the Korean deli a block from my house, a place I'd come three or four days a week for the better part of a year. It was cool inside, although the enormous air conditioner roaring over the door meant the people behind the counter were half shouting to each other. As was the norm for so many places in New York, my loyalty to this bagel shop earned me not so much as a smile when I went up to the counter. A stubbly Korean man I'd seen a few hundred times rubbed his face with his left hand, not looking up from a yellow piece of paper.

"What you wan?"

I signed. "The same thing I always get."

The pen in his right hand didn't move, and he stood there looking down, waiting.

"Bagel. Onion. Cream cheese, not too heavy. Toasted. Coffee, cream and sugar."

My coffee arrived in its little blue-and-white cup, ubiquitous to the city. *We are happy to serve you* was emblazoned on the side. At least the cup was friendly.

A few moments later my bagel was up. I took it and my coffee, braving the heat back to the apartment, where I entered the narrow lobby. I noticed mail poking out the side of my box: a *Time* magazine, two credit card bills, two credit card offers, a coupon flyer, and a thin envelope from Random House. I stared at the Random House envelope. My name was in the center, perfectly typed. I looked around me, at the strange, otherworldly blueness of the lobby, which had inexplicably been tiled in a poolside friendly deep azure. The envelope was thin. Very thin, like there was only a single piece of paper inside of it. I climbed the stairs to my door, laid the mail on the kitchen table.

I wondered if they might say they had liked the book and to call them. But that didn't make sense. I'd included my phone number, of course. Maybe it said a contract would be coming to me if I was interested, but again that seemed like an additional step that a busy company wouldn't bother to take. They'd just call me, wouldn't they? Maybe it was a polite letter rejecting me. That was what it was. Thin, to the point. Because of Rebecca, maybe it was even a personal letter that wasn't just one of their form letter rejections. My mouth had gone dry.

I picked the envelope up and turned it over. I smelled it, set it back down and went to the window, looking out over the back alley, forgetting completely about my breakfast and coffee. I wondered if maybe I should take a walk. But my feet brought me back to the table, and my pinkie was sliding between the flap and the body of the envelope before I even knew what I was doing. And then the letter tumbled out and fluttered to the floor, expertly folded. I leaned down to pick it up. And indeed, it was a single, typed page, hand-signed and formally addressed to me.

Dear Mr. Downing was followed by a few, short few paragraphs of text. It wasn't from Rebecca, who didn't make these kinds of decisions but rather passed them on to her staff.

My eyes dropped from my name, *Dear Mr. Downing*, onto the first paragraph and all the way to the *sincerely*, and then went back two more times. I then carefully folded it back along its seams, placed in its envelope, and put in the top drawer of the tiny desk that doubled as a table for shoes, belts, books to be read, and empty glasses.

I went to the closet and grabbed the backpack with my catering clothes folded inside and, even though I would be at least an hour early, left for work.

Friday

Our Monday meeting, pushed back to Friday, is interminable. I press a finger along my temple in an attempt to gently massage out the fibrous headache that has been there since I woke up. Around the table in Rectangle sit Jen, Jamie, Steve, and me. On the HD TV is the Excel doc that charts our progress. Each person's area of responsibility is listed, and under it what they're tasked to do along with how complete that task is.

Mine looks like this:

Content Marketing	Status Completed
Create and Distribute 2 blogs per week (24 blogs for quarter)	55%
Create December Content Theme Asset: Board Reporting	30%
Create 3 New Interviews & 3 New Customer Case Studies	0%
Support and enable creation of buyer personas, stages, and content matrix	50%
Create Q1 Content Theme Asset: Road Map to Compliance Success	5%
Increase blog subscribers by 3x	20%
Quick fixes to website around traffic paths and common objections	20%
Create and manage content partners	0%

I'm the newest hire and as such go last in these weekly meetings, which means my numbers are the ones that stay on the screen even after we're all done. I've already spent fifteen minutes speaking about the percentages, where I stand on each point, and what I'm planning on doing this week.

"So," Steve is saying, "we had a pretty good week? I apologize for this meeting being, well, almost a week late, but I was in Chicago on Monday and then tied up with the whole Coca-Cola mess after that. Of course we didn't get Coke, which everyone knows, but it's not supposed to be formally announced until Monday by Michael, so keep it between us, even though everyone knows." He smiles but his eyes remain flat and exhausted. "So good job this week, team. It seems like we're building a head of steam to push through some of these sales numbers where we've been static for almost two quarters. Funding for the next cycle is looking strong, and that's in large part because of the work you've all done. Any questions?"

"I've got one," Jamie says, looking sideways at Steve. Her black hair curls up at the edges where it touches her navy blue blouse. "So I did the due diligence on the BDR reports, and they're not following through with the information we're giving them." She pauses and looks around the table. "We're doing *our* part here, but ... "

"That gets complicated, right? We have to be careful not to seem critical of other departments. That's up to Jeff and sales team to work through." He pauses. "But ... it's possible that we're too siloed," he says. "On this team. Maybe we can find a better way to bring our data and resources to help them meet their goals, so it's one team and not lots of small teams." He looks around at us with those flat, tired eyes.

Jamie nods. "Logan's white paper generated," she glances down at her computer, "fifteen leads. Nice work, Logan."

Steve says nothing.

"Thanks," I say, noting Steve's silence.

"Anything else?" Jen asks, the red-rimmed eyes looking desperate to close themselves.

"I know you're pushing it hard, guys," Steve says. "It's not going unnoticed." He hesitates. "I have a surprise for you all, coming soon."

"Oh yes, because surprises are so much fun in startups," Jamie comments.

Jen and I both laugh and Steve shakes his head. "Good surprise," he amends. I know the company sometimes authorizes executives like Steve to do things like buy a half-day a spa for their workers. I presume it's something like this.

"You wanna get lunch?" Jen asks Jamie.

"Done."

I stand and start getting my things together.

"Logan," Steve says.

I look up.

"Stay a minute?"

"Sure."

"And close the door?" I close the door and then dig my notebook back out of my bag and sit down.

"Shoot."

His boyish face is flushed and unhappy. "I have to be frank: your performance is not up to speed." He folds his hands in front of him in a way that makes me think of a high school principal.

"I've been working fifty-hour weeks," I protest, before I have a chance to think about it and respond more professionally.

He cocks a head at the display on the screen looming at one end of the table. "It's not about long hours. It's about getting things done. Your percentages are all very low."

I say nothing and feel my cheeks start to burn.

"But more than that. You're just not taking the initiative the way I was hoping you would. It seems like you don't know what to do sometimes. For instance, when you were working on the last board report, Jen says you didn't get the materials to her in time, and you missed the internal deadline you said you'd meet."

It was Jen who held me up by blowing her deadline, which had forced me to work two days until after seven.

"I know we're all super busy," I say, trying to resist the urge to lay blame on her. "But that's not my memory of how things went down. She had promised to have the work by end of day Tuesday, and I didn't get it until mid-day Thursday."

"I don't want to get into a he-said-she-said," Steve dismisses. "The point is you missed a deadline. You've missed a few and I know you're relatively new, and no one is questioning your writing, which is very good. What's going on, for instance, with the content partnerships?"

There are a few places I've been overwhelmed at work, and one of them is trying to understand how to use the authority I've been given, such as how to work with contractors — professional content providers — who we might pay to write things for us, something totally alien to me. The truth is I don't know what to do there.

Steve unfolds his hands and leans back in his chair.

"With those," I stumble, "those partnerships. I'm, I'm working on that."

"Mmm hmm. We need to turn around the ship." He leans forward and puts both elbows on the table. I know a lot about Steve, actually — where he went to school and grew up, what his college years were like, how he is with his wife. "I'd like to stay married" is a frequent retort when someone jokes he should stand up more to her. I know he has a son but wanted four, that his commute is longer than mine, and that deep down he's a really good guy — a reliable husband and father and a kind human being. We're not friends, but we're friendly, and I decide to stop with the business formality and address him in a more human way.

"I accept that I can do better," I say. "And that I've dropped some balls. The deadlines — *that* I would push back on. I've had trouble getting some of the people on our team to meet the deadlines we agree on, but I do accept that that too is my responsibility."

Steve nods, expressionless.

"But the truth is I'm a lifelong freelancer. I'm used to coming in as an outsider, doing my job, and leaving once the project is complete. It's been an adjustment in some ways, synching up with the culture here, and figuring out a role that lasts longer than a few weeks, or months. I've done the best I can."

He gives me a look like he doesn't understand me. Of course, I should stop here, but I don't.

"What I mean by that is Jen and Jamie and you and everyone here all come from corporate backgrounds — I'm a bit of a fish out of water, which I think my background showed." I pause and look him squarely in the eyes. "You hired me, after all."

No change in expression.

"Ater some meetings I'm not sure what I should do. It's not always clear to me." I swallow. Steve is still sitting immobile.

"I could probably use some mentoring in some ways from you, a little guidance to figure out how I might do my job better. So maybe, just for a little bit, we could work together on that, like after a meeting to make sure I've got the right order of things that need to be done."

He nods once, sharply, and doesn't lift his eyes for a moment. His face is very red.

"Well," he says, abruptly standing and beginning to gather his things. "So you could start by writing a blog from someone else's perspective, one of the EVPs. Like we discussed. Weeks ago. Or you could set up a content partnership this week, like we already discussed and that I green-lighted. Weeks ago. You could focus on the content theme for

Q4, which has been on deck for a month. And that we discussed weeks ago." He says all these things without looking at me. "There's a lots of things you could have been doing," he says, "without my input. It's called doing your job."

He walks briskly out he door and I stay seated, looking after him.

Summer, 1996

The carriage was white with matching seats, an embroidered blue blanket — unnecessary in the summer afternoon air — draped over the back, and plastic flowers sprouting along the rear. We were being pulled by a beautiful lumbering draft horse. Our driver, a loquacious woman of about thirty with short blonde hair, had finally given us a moment to ourselves after I'd shot her a look.

"It's been so cool," Carissa was saying, "I *love* this weather!"

"It's amazing," I agreed.

"So what made you decide to get a carriage," Carissa asked as we crossed the Bow Bridge in Central Park, water on either side of us. The trees were lush and full and the thickness of them dimmed the distant sound of the city. "It's not like you."

"I wanted to celebrate," I said, smiling.

Carissa looked at me, her eyes playful and loving and curious.

"Random House got back to me," I said.

Her eyes went wide and I nodded and laughed.

"They want to publish me."

"OH MY GOD!" She jumped onto my lap, straddling me and kissing me and talking all at once. "OH MY GOD! And you were going to take a job for them as an *editor*!"

"Not really."

"For like two seconds you were!"

The driver of the carriage turned around and smiled. "Congratulations!"

"Thank you!"

"Oh my god, babe! Holy shit, you did it. You're not a pretentious *aspiring* artist anymore, you're a pretentious *actual* artist!"

I laughed again. "It's true."

"When did you find out?"

"Two days ago."

She punched me playfully in the arm. "And you didn't tell me until *today*?"

"I know, I know!"

"Hardly the fight you were expecting! See, life can be easy and fun if you let it."

"That's true," I admitted. She slid off my lap and we turned to face each other on the seat. "Maybe life isn't a battle," I laughed.

"So what's next?"

"I don't know," I said. "I mean, I have to go in and meet them, sign a contract, go through edits — all that kind of stuff."

"That's so amazing. So that's why you wanted to ride in the carriage?"

"Yup." We were rounding the Bethesda Fountain. I pulled a ring from my jeans pocket. "And to ask you to marry me, with this silver ring." I paused. "Gold was a bit pricey."

Carissa's eyes narrowed for a moment, and then she put a hand to cover her mouth.

"I can't really get on a knee since I'm sitting down already, but will you marry me? Carissa, will you be my wife?"

Tears came to her eyes. "Of course! Of course I will!"

I slipped the plain silver band around her ring finger. She looked at it, full of wonder and awe, as if it had come from Tiffany's and were encrusted in precious jewels, and then threw her arms around me. "I love you so much," she cried into my ear.

"I couldn't do it without you," I said. "Any of it. I wouldn't want to. Wherever this ride is going to take me, I want you to be at my side."

The driver, unable to container herself any longer, turned to face us. "I've always wanted for a couple to get engaged in my carriage," she gushed, "and this guy was prepared!" She leaned down and pulled out a picnic basket with champagne and two glasses, popped the cork and poured, and passed them back to us, all the while navigating the carriage.

"How ... " Carissa began.

"I set it up last night," I said, smiling. "After work. I brought Donna here the champagne and glasses and arranged for her to pick us up today at two."

"Baby, that is so romantic. So thoughtful. So sneaky!"

I grinned at her. "Isn't it?"

"Oh Christ, but don't let it go to your head!"

"Too late," I said, and raised my glass. "Here's to us, and to following our dreams."

"To dreams," Carissa said, wiping her cheeks. "And us." We clinked classes and drank, and then Carissa settled into me. I put my right arm around her and felt the weight and warmth of her body leaning into mine.

"Take us around the park again, will you, Donna? And then drop us off near Sixty-second and Fifth? We have dinner plans over there."

I felt Carissa smile, and she held out her left hand, fingers splayed, looking at the plain silver ring in the full light of the summer afternoon.

Monday

I come in to work early today, hoping to make a better impression. Steve is on the phone but he nods at me. Jen looks up tiredly when I sit down.

"Hey," she says, "how was your weekend?"

"Good. Went out to dinner on Saturday."

She smiles. "It's been a long time since Paul and I have been able to have a nice dinner out."

"You have two kids, right?" I ask. "A newborn and a four-year-old?"

She nods. "Handful, for both of us."

"I bet."

"You're engaged?"

"Yup."

"Planning on having a family?"

"That was the idea."

She looks at me oddly. "Was?"

I smile awkwardly. "*Is* the idea. Freudian slip."

Jen laughs. "Oh, I get it. Be careful; once you're in, it's hard to go out."

I laugh. I decide to go through the list Steve gave me on Friday and get as much of it done as needed to turn my performance around. I contact one of the EVPs in the company to let her know I'm writing a blog in her name and request a time when we might meet. I email one of the content providers Steve wanted me to work with and request an interview as soon as he can become available. I then research our content theme for the upcoming month. I set up an appointment with a new hire, a young woman who happens to be an expert in some of the programs I'm struggling to understand and use.

When I push back from my desk a few hours later, it occurs to me I haven't eaten or had my second cup of coffee. I'm not feeling very hungry, so instead I decide to stretch my legs by walking over to a coffee shop a few blocks away.

The small hipster coffee shop just off of Broadway and Ninth. It's a big space, bright and airy and half a story down from the curb. The floor is a worn blonde wood, the walls a vibrant red, and ample outside seating overlooks a busy street. A gas fire pit in the courtyard throws out heat against the cold afternoon air.

I get coffee in a sixteen-ounce glass and sit outside at a four-top, as most of the seats are empty. There is a couple nearby; she's facing me and, even though she's seated, I can tell she's tall, long legs thrown across one another under the table. Her hair is an unmanaged chaos of dark curls. An almond-shaped face frames Caribbean-green eyes that are large and alert. Green eyes, I reflect. They're rare, and they never fail to make me think of Carissa.

The woman's leather coat is ankle-length. She wears anklets, bracelets, and necklaces, along with rings of many shapes and sizes. Combat boots, their soles turned up toward me, are worn through at the heel in a way that suggests she drags her feet when she walks.

I look away and take a few sips of my coffee, watch the traffic go by, check my phone, and then finally look at the houses across the street. But when my gaze inevitably goes back to her, those green eyes shift away from mine just before there's contact. The young man she's with is talking intermittently, as if he's afraid he might say the wrong thing.

As I'm nearing the bottom of my coffee, they stand. He kisses her and then leaps over the short wall to the sidewalk. She pulls out her phone and leans into it. I glance at my empty pint glass. Even though I should get back to work, I decide to go back in for a refill. When I take my seat outside once more, I put my feet up into a chair and look in her direction. She immediately looks away but then almost as quickly brings her eyes back toward mine in a kind of defiance.

"Nice boots," I offer, before my increasing heartbeat can sabotage my mouth.

"Thanks," she says without looking away or smiling. "They're good for kicking ass."

I try not to let my surprise show. "Indeed. That was your boyfriend or partner or, well, whatever?"

She nods. "He's straight out of nowhere. Like a shooting star. Especially while I have had two blazing middle fingers up to the world of weak-willed men."

Again I stifle my surprise. I sit up, almost knocking my coffee over. I look at her a little sheepishly.

"That's been your experience of most men." I decide to make it a statement instead of a question.

She snorts at me.

"What about that one?" I nod my head toward the short wall the young man just leapt over.

She shakes her head. "Why don't they use their words? Why?" She shakes a mass of brown hair off her shoulder, some of the necklaces jingling under the motion. Her green eyes haven't left mine once, and in that moment I'm not even sure if she's blinked yet. "You're using *your* words. It's not so hard. The world is full of fucking words, like these. You put them together, in a certain kind of order, and you *convey* shit. You can even *talk* about things. Like feelings. Even *your* feelings."

"Words are good."

She gives me what I think is a mock look of warning. "These child-men want to run back to safety as soon as a strong woman stands up to them. Fuck 'em."

I laugh, since I'm not sure how else to respond. I guess she's probably twenty-seven or so, give or take a year. "And him?"

"Him?" She looks away for the first time, down the sidewalk where he went. I blink a few times and exhale. "Yeah, he's a good egg. He's doing a pretty good job of it, so long as he remembers to use his words."

"It's kinda tough being a fella," I say. "There's no room for the Steve McQueen archetype in today's world." She nods. "You don't know who he is, do you? Steve McQueen?"

A grin comes to her long and full lips, painted red and cracking in a dozen places.

"You have no idea the door you just opened." She puts those big combat boots under herself and sits up.

"Oh?"

"No idea." She takes her phone out and starts scrolling through it, the green eyes flickering past images I can't see, the cracked-lipped grin fixed. "Come here." She pats the seat next to her. I do as I'm told. She then smacks the phone down on the metal table, facing me, the smile expanding into a victorious grin.

I look down to see one of the iconic shots of Steve McQueen: a gravelly and handsome face resting in an open helmet, cigarette hanging out of the center of his mouth, the eyes pinched and, in black and white, startlingly grey. Two gloved hands are clasping a strap under his lifted chin.

I look up.

"I drew that," she says as soon as my eyes touch hers, "six years ago, at the ripe old age of twenty-two."

"You ... drew *that*?" I say, genuinely shocked.

She leans forward on the metal table, elbows down. "Charcoal. Took me a month. I *know* who Steve *fucking* McQueen is, and yes — to your point, none of the men my age could so much as light one of his cigarettes without shitting in their britches."

"Britches?"

"Words," she replies, sitting back. "Powerful things." She points one long finger down at her phone. I notice the nails are cut functionally short and the cuticles chewed. "That is a *man*."

I nod. "Steve McQueen was the real deal. Burned his candle at both ends, the way of all real men of that era."

"Alea," she says. It takes me a moment to realize that's her name.

"Logan."

"So what's your story, Logan?"

I sit back too. Now there are many ways to answer that question, of course. There's the polite way, to state your job and your idealized relationship status, like "I'm in the executive suite at a tech start up and engaged to a cutting-edge coach." And there's the middle way, along the lines of "I'm working a job here in town, a startup, and working on a book for the first time in a long time, and trying to get clear on what's going on with my relationship." And there's the real way, where you just tell the truth and let it all land wherever it may, like vomit across a wall instead of neatly into a toilet.

"I used to be an artist," I say. "Got a book published years back. Novel. Won some awards for the words in it, and even made me some money. Started it in New York City in 1995 when I was just out of school and finally found a home for it. Since then I've made money as a freelance writer, but I took a job a few months back, a full time adult job, with a tech company." I pause. "I hate it, actually."

"That's no surprise," she states. "No more books?"

"Stillborn," I say.

"Yeah, and that doesn't fit into the 'better to have loved and lost' shit, does it?"

"No. Plus I'm engaged, but that's not going so well either." That was the first time I'd said those words out loud to anyone.

She stares unblinkingly at me.

"I'm in a creative rut, I'm getting older, and I'm not sure what I'm supposed to do with the rest of my life. I'm a cliché of an early midlife crisis."

"If you say so." She looks at me with a slight smile. "And not *that* early."

I smile.

"But you gotta pay your bills."

"Yeah. And somewhere, somehow, I started to make compromises. You know; you've done it with men."

She nods. "Why did you take the job?" she says at last.

"Money. Plus the freelance game starts to get old after a few ... decades."

"Artists don't generally fit well inside of corporate boxes, no matter how brightly painted they are."

I feel stupidly flattered at being called an artist by this strangely intense young woman.

"That's part of why I'm back to bodywork after a year of just painting. But I'm re-strategizing ... and I plan on eventually just painting again. It's often the way of it. I don't think I know a single artist who's had a straight-upward financial trajectory. Which I partially accept. But it also motivates me to think outside the box as far as income sources and possibilities with what I do."

"Yeah — I think that's smart. How do we make art *and* live well?"

"You figure it out, you be sure to let me know."

"Well," I say, finishing the last of my coffee. "I should probably get back to the office, as dreadful a sentence as that is."

She laughs. "At least you know how to use your words, Logan. Well done. Feelings and everything. Enjoy the day as best you can."

I turn to leave, and she speaks to my back.

"You know, you carry any more tension in those shoulders and your head is going to pop right off of your neck."

I turn around. "What?"

"Tension. Body worker, remember?" She points at herself. "That thing I just told you about myself?"

"Ah yes, that."

"You keep it up, and maybe you take out a nice person just trying to enjoy her coffee."

"Take out? What?"

"Take out." She says the words slowly. "Sure. Think about it: all that tension and your head blows off and then what? It smacks me right in *my* head, and now your tension has just killed someone." She raises her eyebrows. "And made a mess for the poor barista."

"Oh," I say, stupidly.

"So I'm busy as fuck," she says, "because I'm good at what I do. At bodywork."

"I bet."

"I say that not to brag," she continues, "but as a statement of fact. I'm usually booked for two months out. It's just," she wiggles her phone at me, "right now, as you're standing there, I got notified of a cancelation tomorrow, my 7:15. Last one of the night," she says, "and only forty-five minutes, which probably isn't enough, but if you want it, it's yours."

"Oh ... can you hold it for me?"

She shakes her head. "Sorry, cowboy. I'm the artist; you want the receptionist for that."

"Oh?"

"There's this thing called the In-ter-net. Lotus Massage of Denver."

"I'll book it," I say, not at all sure that I will.

"What's your last name?"

"Downing."

She winks one of her green eyes at me and then looks back at her phone.

Summer, 1996

Engaged?" Jackson said. I saw sarcasm fire behind his eyes but, as he looked from me to Carissa, he checked it. "I'm happy for you guys. Been married four years myself." He was wearing his usual denim ménage.

"Aw," Carissa replied, squeezing my hand, "that's so sweet."

Franklin's apartment was only four hundred square feet, but the north-facing window that took up almost the entire wall overlooked the Chrysler Building in a spectacular fashion. Hardwood floors and high ceilings, along with a fireplace filled with candles, made it seem bigger than it was. Music came from tiny Bose speakers tucked unobtrusively into the corners. As a painter, his needs were simple: a pullout leather couch, a long narrow end table, a wooden chair he had pulled from a dumpster and painted himself, and his easel. The latter had a mostly finished painting displayed on it, a depiction of three angels falling through flames and into hell.

"She used to do modeling in college," Jackson was saying, "but now she's in finance. Here." He took his wallet out, the brown leather worn nearly through in patches. He pulled a photograph showing an attractive woman with brown hair and brown eyes from an inside pouch.

"Very beautiful," Carissa said. "You're a lucky man."

"Not bad for a ball and chain," he said, unable to contain his sarcasm any longer. "She's got a velvet cuff, at least."

"Tell me about this," Alejandro asked Franklin, looking at the painting. "What's the inspiration? It's darker than your others I've seen." Alejandro wore a royal blue sports coat with a black collarless shirt underneath that opened to show off a rich tapestry of chest hair.

"Inferno," Franklin answered, "and the Gates to Hell."

"I see the Rodin influence," Alejandro replied.

I edged closer.

"So it's a modern interpretation," Franklin said. "The handsome one is pride. The muscular one is hard work. And the cherub-faced one is hope. At top, instead of the thinker, it's fate. Below isn't hell, its obscurity."

Alejandro seemed to contemplate Franklin with a combination of love and awe. "Fuck."

"Obscurity," I repeated. "A fate worse than hell?"

"Brilliant," Alejandro breathed.

Franklin turned to me. "For some."

"Was that painting in your show at the Whitney?" I asked.

"No, I just finished it last week."

Alejandro folded his arms. "I see. Was it influenced by what happened there?"

"What happened there?" I asked.

"Remember that line to get in?"

I laughed. There had been a line that went halfway down the block. We'd all assumed Franklin had somehow broken into fame overnight and the lined-up people were all waiting to see his work. But it turned out that MTV was filming an episode of *The Real World* in the museum and hundreds had shown up to watch the filming, not to see my brother's art opening.

"But his show had pretty good attendance," I noted.

Franklin merely shrugged. "It was okay. I mean, maybe a hundred people came through." He took a sip of his drink.

"Well," Alejandro said, lifting his glass and changing the subject, "cheers to you. It's huge what you've done so far. I'm in awe."

"Thank you," Franklin said, smiling, his blue eyes happy but, I thought, worn. "And your photography exhibition is, what, a month away? At NYU?"

There was a nod and a tip of an imaginary hat. "You'll all be expected to attend."

"The man of the hour, however," said Franklin, "is my little brother, Logan Downing, who just signed a contract with Random House for his first ever novel. *And* got engaged."

"Hey," Jackson called, "don't get nuts on the celebrations. Wait till my wife gets here or she'll be pissed!"

"Sure. This is just a primer." Franklin raised his glass of whiskey and we all raised ours. "It's amazing, bro. Carissa, congratulations. Your world is about to change in ways you can't imagine."

"Cheers to the engagement," Jackson said. "But that book thing. Too much luck in one family. Can't one of you guys make your living in an honest way?"

"I haven't been paid a nickel yet," I said, "if that helps. I'm still catering to pay the bills."

"At least you're earning your keep for a little bit longer. You make any money selling books?"

"You have to sell a lot of books to make any real money, and that's pretty rare."

"So don't quit your day job. You're a step ahead of that no-good brother of yours, who never had a real one."

Jackson's wife came a half-hour later, and then Carissa's roommate Amy joined us. Even Franklin's girlfriend, the reclusive Lily, came, although being a yogi she didn't drink anything except filtered water. More than her discipline, I admired her ability to tolerate a room full of drunks.

From Franklin's apartment we left and went down the block to a bar that had managed to get a full-sized yellow school bus inside. The fine wine and whiskey gave way to shots of tequila and longneck bottles. Seven of us piled into a tiny booth meant to seat four, and Alejandro pulled out a small antique camera.

"Let's do this," he said. "First the brothers." He clamped his cigarette between his teeth.

Franklin and I leaned in, cheek to cheek, with my face more of a leer and his more of a dignified smile. The flash went off.

"Now the married couple." Jackson and his wife kissed across the table. A few photos were snapped.

"Now the newly engaged ones." Carissa hopped nimbly onto my lap and, at the moment I yelled out in mock surprise, Alejandro snapped the picture.

"Lastly, all of us. Hey!" he yelled at the table nearby. "Take a photo?"

A stout man in a baseball cap and Mets T-shirt lumbered over. "Where do I press?"

"The same place you do on every camera." Alejandro then launched his small five-foot-five frame onto the table, arching his back and sliding directly toward Jackson. At the moment of impact, the flash went off.

Tuesday Night

I park on a residential street a few blocks off an industrialized intersection in South Denver, where a green house is set back from the road. It's modest and welcoming, the kind of place you'd expect an elderly aunt to live. As I step onto the porch, I pass winter pansies arranged in planters.

Inside, the house appears as I imagined from the outside. There are fabrics and fountains for mood, low lights and gentle music. An attractive woman looks up from behind the desk as I enter, her dark skin blending into the shadows behind her. There are bookshelves on my right and, in what would be the living room to my left, couches and chairs for waiting.

"You're to see Alea?" she asks, smiling. Hoop earrings with tiny pink crystals dangle.

I nod.

"And you filled out your forms online, I see."

"As told."

"So all you gotta do, love, is take a seat and wait for her. She should be out in just a moment."

I go into the other room and sit on a couch that threatens to swallow me. I adjust toward a firmer outer edge, cross my legs, and then uncross them. Just as I'm wondering how to look relaxed, even considering picking up one of the magazines laid out on the table in front of me, there's movement from the shadows. Alea emerges, eyes first, followed by a rouge skirt and black loose-fitting top. Brown hair spirals down around her face and a silver snake encircles her left biceps.

"You're up," she says, and indicates I'm to follow her.

We move to a small room behind the reception desk. Although it's night, the windows are heavily curtained. The room is painted in purples and rich reds and is dimly lit with half a dozen candles adding their uncertain light to two tiny strings of Christmas lights. A Moroccan-themed mirror hangs on one wall, metal with semi-precious stones encircling the reflection. She comes in behind me and closes the door, so that when I turn around she's standing very close. I glance down to see her toes, painted purple, spreading out over a Persian rug.

"So I read your form," she says in a professional manner at odds with how close we're standing. "Anything else you want to add to it?" Her eyes are like an ocean.

"My back is tight," I mumble. "Lower back. Holds a lot of tension."

"Mmm mm," she says. "And in those shoulders." An arm uncoils from her side and rubs my shoulder for a moment.

"Right."

"Get naked, lie down on your belly, and breathe. I'll be right back."

My breath hitches at the word *naked*. She steps into the hallway and closes the door behind her. I strip off my clothes, folding them neatly on an antique-looking chair, and lie down on a table heated from underneath. I pull a blanket over my legs and to the small of my back. Just as I'm settling in, there's a knock. She steps in without waiting for a response.

"And preference on music?" I hear her murmur.

"No."

"And pressure?"

"Hard is good."

She lets out a sort of chuckle. "Sure, but we'll see if you can handle it."

Tribal drumming fills the room and then warm hands press on my shoulders. I jump, and hear a laugh.

"Easy. I won't bite."

I laugh too.

"That costs extra." A pause. "I'm a little surprised to see you."

"Oh? You told me to use that Internet thingie."

"I did. I thought I might have scared you away."

"Hardly."

She moves up to my neck and her thumbs press into me with a pointed intensity. I have to breathe deeply to let her penetrate without wincing.

"So," I say, speaking in a slightly muffled voice, looking down through the massage table cushion. "What's your story? What's with the neo-pagan confidence?"

She snickers. "I was raised fundamentalist."

"Oh?"

"Oh is right. It's a sigh-worthy fact that is constant and unoriginal. But to be honest, had I not been internally struck by lightening a few years back, I never would have gotten out."

"How did you break free?"

"I was older, almost twenty-four, before I saw through the construct. Then my world fell apart."

"You were a fundamentalist Christian until you were twenty-four?" It's hard to resist the temptation to turn around to just talk to her and forget the massage but, as that thought arises, she digs deep into my lower back.

I groan, then say, "Your intensity and confidence made me think you'd been free your whole life."

She moves to my right side. "I suppose nobody is ready until they're ready. Now I'm just another sinner. It hurts. When that comes from family. Especially because I see how much more is available to a questioning mind. I can't help but wish more for them." She paused. "I suppose they would say the same thing about my salvation."

"I was raised Catholic. Been fighting shame around my body and sexuality my whole life. Makes me angry sometimes too."

"My anger is because I suffered at the hands of those beliefs for so long. Had to do some hardcore inner work to recover myself. Which is kind of where my boyfriend is now. He's me three years ago. Which is part of where I'm helping him out. But part of where I'm frustrated sometimes. I want to get him more into his body."

"Your body should get him into his."

She laughs. "It does help. He's come a long way in a couple months. I'm a pro-sin priestess. Isn't it crazy how, even when you learn this stuff later in life, the developmental programming is still etched in there?"

"It's astounding. I used to purge my stuff through my writing. I guess I am doing that again."

"I purge the shame through my art. Well, and through fucking people."

I smile into the floor.

"Sorry — too much?"

"No, just what I needed, actually."

"What's that?"

"A reminder."

"Good. Now shut the fuck up and let me do my work."

A few squirts of oil and thumbs and palms begin pressing, turning, and moving across my back, much faster than before. Her touch is strong but careful, staying just below what might make me wince.

She works her way down to my mid-back, then moves to my right side and down, where she uncovers my right leg fully, tucking the sheet between my legs as she works down to my foot. She moves over to the other foot, then works her way up the left leg. By the time she reaches my shoulders again, I'm entering the in-between realm of bliss, fighting to stay in my body and not float off into a trance of pleasure.

"I need you to turn over, love," she whispers, and I do.

My eyes are closed. My left arm, palm up, goes off the table. She moves into that hand and I can feel it pressing somewhere into her waist. As she steps again I realize my hand is resting between her legs. I turn my palm to cup the inside of her thigh, gently and through the fabric of her skirt, almost not touching her at all. She presses into that hand, increasing the pressure before she steps away, taking my hand in hers and working on my fingers one at a time. Then she works the other side. Finally, she is standing behind me. With my eyes still closed I feel her hair come across my face as her hands slide down my chest toward my belly, moving along the lines of the muscles, her face now so close to mine I can smell her, feel her breath across my neck. I lift my chest toward her, inhaling deeply, and sense her lips just above mine, those cracked, full red lips, and I lift my own into the air, my nose in the deep curve of her neck. Our lips touch. I stretch my hands around behind me to her sides, and she turns my head to one side and rubs down my neck with a thumb and then takes my hands in hers and puts them back at my side.

"So we're out of time," she whispers.

It takes me a minute to understand what she's just said. "What? Really?"

"Over by ten, actually. It was a little too good to end right on time."

"Wow," I manage. It seems like it's been five minutes. Or a thousand.

"Take your time getting dressed," she says, back into her professional tone. "I'll be back in."

She's gone before I can move. I slide off the table and slowly, awkwardly, put my clothes on. Just as I'm getting my second sock onto my foot she comes in with a glass of water. I take the water and drink some of it, then offer it to her. She smiles and drinks, and I stand up. She's nearly my height.

"So you're all set," she says, stepping into the main room.

"Thanks," I reply.

"Next time book a longer slot. We didn't have enough time."

"We did not." I look around the room and only the receptionist is there, reading with her back to us.

I take Alea's hand and guide her back into the massage room. I push her against the wall and pull her mane of hair to one side, kissing her deeply and inhaling the fragrance of her before gently biting her neck. She moans and her hand takes a fistful of my hair. I look into her almond-shaped green eyes and we kiss again. I run my hands along her waist, her belly, the rise of her breasts, and her neck.

"I'm glad you pulled me in here," she whispers. "But you need to go. We're keeping Juliet waiting here."

"The receptionist?"

"The stone cold goddess who works behind the desk."

"Right." I step out into the hallway and look back to see her lopsided grin before she disappears into the room.

"How was your bodywork?" Juliet asks. I can't tell if she's aware of what's happening or not. I kind of think she must be.

"I don't know what planet I'm on," I say.

"She has that effect on people. Here's your receipt. Tip is on the bottom. Charge to the same card we have online?"

"Sure." What does one tip for that kind of massage, I wonder. I scrawl $25.

"Bathroom?"

"In the hallway."

I find the bathroom. As I turn on the light I'm surprised at the man who is looking back at me. He's flushed and relaxed and alive, and the bruises under his eyes are gone. He looks happy and confused and a little afraid, so I throw so water onto his face and leave without looking at him again. A few moments later I'm back in my car.

When I pull up in front of my house an hour later, the lights are out and I find myself hoping she's gone to bed. I quietly close the car door, slinging my bag across my shoulder. I slip into the unlocked house. The downstairs is quiet and dark, her dinner dishes stacked neatly next to the sink. My dirty dishes from the morning – one plate and one mug – are still in the sink. Everything is clean and ordered and in its place;

the couch has a brown blanket draped in a perfect rectangle across its back and there is a neat line of shoes parallel to the door. I climb the stairs far enough to see darkness under the master bedroom door, so I go back downstairs, turn on a light, and run my hand through my hair.

I feel an aliveness in my body. I sense that something has been ignited inside me and is now burning, but I can't tell if it's more like a candle or a fuse, and in that moment I don't much care what it is or what might get burned down or blown apart.

I go to my study and take out my laptop. I'm inspired, I realize, to write about the time, ten years ago, when I had known a woman similar to Alea. My hands move across the keyboard no longer wanting — no longer needing — to write about Carissa and New York City twenty years before. I still don't know what it is I'm writing, or why.

Philadelphia, 2002

The tidy fieldstone row homes leaned against one another, shoulder to shoulder. I walked two-way streets wide enough for only one car, a casualty of having been laid down in a time when the laborers who traveled them would either be walking on foot or riding a horse.

I came to a dead-end lane where, at the bottom of the L-shaped street, a pub squatted on the ground floor of a corner house. It sat next to rusting railway tracks that would take you to downtown Philadelphia from the gentrifying neighborhood of Manayunk. A century before, Manayunk had been a bastion of industry, with factories positioned near the Schuylkill River, which flowed eastward toward the city proper. Workers were housed in the narrow, cramped row homes and, for two generations, had provided strong American labor. But when the rustbelt formed and grew during the seventies, rotting the cores of cities like

Pittsburg and Trenton, the neighborhood of Manayunk had atrophied into a dangerous place to live, a place of motorcycle gangs, corner bars, cheap meth, and a nearly empty main street.

I had already left New York, breaking my lease and moving with little thought. Within a few years, as New York became more and more expensive, artists and young creatives began flowing southward into the much more affordable and livable Philadelphia. And so the shithole I'd moved into was turning, in just a few years, into an upwardly mobile neighborhood.

A strip of meth houses sat across the railway from the pub on the opposite side of the tracks. They were connected by a pedestrian bridge, decaying as if from disease. Metal flakes littered its walkway like sloughed-off skin, and the rust was so cancerous in some places that light shone through what should have been two inches of steel.

Only a few years before, the pub had been a biker hangout known for the reliably crappy meth dealt out of it. Patrons would pull their Harleys inside through a side door where they could get drunk while working on their bikes.

The place had gone through a strange evolution since then, from dive bar to pub. In an attempt to drive out the bikers and bring in a more sophisticated clientele, the new owner had stopped serving any kind of cheap or popular beer. Although he now served some of the finest and most exotic beers one could hope to find anywhere in the country, the space itself still had holes in the ceiling, bathrooms with yellowed urinals, and graffiti-covered walls. Ceiling fans turned with broken or missing blades, dizzy and off balance. The generation-old wallpaper had long before been stained the tan of cigarette smoke and nicotine. Every night, a smoke eater over the bar worked noisily to clear the smoke but mostly seemed just to push it around; every morning, a gray mop was dragged across a gray tiled floor. The bar, known as the

Dead End Pub, was a fixture in this neighborhood, still half working class and half bohemian, and one of the few places where roofers and contractors would sit next to graduate students and musicians, forming friendships across lines that were growing blurrier as we edged into the twenty-first century.

I walked up the three concrete steps and pushed through the screen door and into the pub. As was typical that time of day, a dozen blue-collar men just off work sat at the bar. These were carpenters and plumbers, maintenance men and bus drivers. I knew that by seven they would be gone and the younger, hipper crowd would have started to take their places.

The bar was on my left as I came in, a hodgepodge of a structure repaired and added onto half a dozen times over fifty years. It ran the length of the main room. Behind it were dirty mirrors, photos of drunk patrons, and, of course, a hundred or so various bottles of booze. There was a middle room into which a pool table had been squeezed, then a back room and lounge, full of mismatched donated furniture, and finally the entrance to the absurdly tiny kitchen where I worked.

"Logan," a man said. He was a squat painter, gray of face and hair and eyes, with a white painter's cap pulled down tight. His overalls were covered in a hundred different splashes of color.

"Hey Mike."

"You make me some wings?" He leaned back in his chair.

"Sure, man. Gimme ten to get the fryers warmed up and I'll bring 'em out."

"You're a doll."

"Fuck you."

He laughed, throaty and rough, lighting a cigarette as I passed him.

My shift started at five, and the spring sun was beaming in through the red and white checkered curtains on the only south-facing window. I nodded to the bartender, a thin and beautiful brunette as reserved in her mannerisms as a mannequin. Long accustomed to unwanted attention by men, especially the ones whose tongues were loosened by the booze she was serving, she lived behind a lattice of detached coldness.

"Hey Marcie," I said. Her blue eyes flickered up from a book.

"Hey."

"Hungry?"

"Nope. Maybe later."

I nodded, walking from the brightly lit front room to the darker middle room and then to the back room, as windowless as the kitchen behind it.

The kitchen was about three feet wide and ten feet long, with two fryers, one set of burners, a gas grill on one side, two restaurant fridges that doubled as cutting boards, and a sink at one end to hand-wash the dirty dishes. It was exactly wide enough for one person, so long as the person was height-weight appropriate. Everything was stained in grease.

It was a full time job and I pulled down two hundred and fifty bucks a week in cash, including complimentary food and booze. It wasn't much but it kept me free when the sun was up so I could use the best part of the day to work on my next book.

I was writing about the changing world I saw. Growing up, the rules were simple: go to college, get a degree, and find a job. My mother had often told me that an education was the one thing the world could never take from you, but her bootstrap mentality hid a dying truism around class. Education as a means to affluence, while once true, was being overturned by an upstart novelty known as the Internet. The whole world was changing, with blue chip companies going under because they were trying to keep up with dotcoms that had produced nothing but ballooning stock prices and promises of future windfalls.

Then a few Saudi nationals had flown jets into two buildings in downtown Manhattan and the dotcom world imploded. The easy money of the late nineties turned out to not be so easy and, while blue chips had rallied and everyone had taken a collective, skeptical breath, it was obvious that something had broken in the world.

It was a quiet Tuesday night. A few orders came back, but I mostly sat on one of the refrigerators and read. A little after seven, I stretched and walked out through the lounge past the unused pool table. The bar, now dark and looking more in its element, had a dozen people spread across it. Janice Joplin sang from the jukebox while the TV silently played a Phillies game.

"Hey," John said.

"Hey," I replied.

He was a totem of a bar owner, a slab of a man with black hair falling to his shoulders. His ample gut and double chin showed the cost of easy access to fine brews and spirits and fried foods. Despite that and the second-hand smoke, he exuded the health and strength of a man who spent his days working in sun-kissed fields. When the occasional bar fight broke out, he moved in like a world-weary parent separating toddlers, pulling men off their feet and pushing them out the bar's door with an almost casual distain.

"You getting any writing in back there?"

I laughed. "There's not enough room for my pen and me in that kitchen."

A grunted laugh.

I took a seat at the bar. John was standing at the waitress' section directly to my right, blocking it entirely.

"So what's it about?" His voice was a baritone.

"What?"

"The next book. People say you won't talk about it."

I smiled. "I never talk about unfinished books. It dilutes the energy."

"Not very good for pre-sales."

I laughed again. "I suppose not."

"Yo John," a man called from the other end of the bar.

"Hey Bill."

"Made you those mix CDs," Bill said, setting a stack of them on the bar. "Rockabilly. Lots of shit for your next road trip."

"Cool."

Marcie, who had been standing at that end, grabbed the CDs and walked back to John.

"Nice," John called. "Three days in the car. Good tunes are essential. Thanks."

At half past midnight I cleaned the kitchen, although with all that caked-on grease everywhere, the operation required a Zen-like lack of attachment to results. With no late-night orders, I shut down promptly at one and sat down at the bar to drink my two shift beers.

"What are you reading?" I asked Marcie.

"*Blindness*," she replied without looking up.

"Any good?"

She looked up briefly, without a smile. "Yes."

I nodded and sipped my beer. "Maybe I could borrow it when you're done."

She was reading again. "I'll be done in two or three days. Will leave it behind the bar."

"Roger that."

I sat in silence. A few other patrons talked quietly among themselves. I left the pub a little before two. My walk took me up a narrow, steep street and across a main drag and then down to a row of homes where I lived in a small flat at the back of one. My flat had hardwood floors, an ancient stove, and a bedroom the size of a prison cell, but it was cheap and quiet and close to work, and I did my writing in the large, sunny kitchen on a plastic Macintosh PowerBook 520c laptop.

I went to open the fridge, a giant antique, catching sight of the photo of Carissa pinned under a magnet there. I had taken the picture of her in New York. Her green eyes were looking to the right of the photo and her lips opening into a smile. She looked full of mischief.

"Hey," I said to her, opening the fridge and grabbing a beer. "I bet you would love the bar where I work. Would be a lot more fun if you'd meet me there for a drink when I got off work."

I stripped out of my stinking clothes, put on some clean sweat pants and a T-shirt, and sat down on my worn couch to read for another half hour before going to bed.

Philadelphia, 2003

That February in Philly was cloudy and sullen and, even when the sun did manage to come through, it hugged the horizon, hoarding warmth to itself. The shadowed city always seemed damp; sleet, rain, and wet snow falling intermittently.

The train emerged from a veil of drizzle, rumbling toward the station through early morning mists. I found a window seat and rested my head, watching as the city's silhouette began to slide past in grays. Philly gave way to New Jersey, the land morphing from industrial and rusting to bucolic and suburban and then, as we neared Trenton, back again. I was in my best clothes, which meant the ones that showed the least amount of wear.

I was headed to an interview for a freelance job with an advertising agency in Manhattan, one of the larger ones in the city, J/MA. The man I was supposed to meet, Chris, had told me point blank he was concerned I was under-qualified and it was only because of Alejandro's strong and passionate recommendation that he had agreed to interview me at all.

With my second novel nearly finished, I figured I could transition to life as a freelance writer in the interim between finishing the book and it coming out. The restaurant business was getting old.

In the distance, the skyline of Manhattan emerged. Without the Twin Towers to mark its southern tip, the city looked at once familiar and foreign. And then the buildings vanished as we entered the long tunnel to Penn Station. Ten minutes later I was disgorged onto the sidewalk. I checked my watch: 10:15. I had forty-five minutes before the interview, so I went to the nearest pay phone, dropped in a quarter, and dialed my brother's apartment.

"Hey Franklin," I said, putting my free finger into my right ear to cut off the sound of traffic.

"Hey man."

"Interview is at eleven; after that, I'm free, like I said yesterday. I'll give you a buzz when I get out so we can decide where to meet up. Doubt the interview will be more than forty minutes, but don't know what to expect." I paused. "Lunch at twelve thirty seems a safe bet."

"Cool man. My day is free. Working in the studio."

"Isn't your whole apartment a studio?"

"Yeah, but it's *the* studio when I'm painting."

We laughed and hung up. I pulled out a small address book that was tucked into my back pocket and flipped to Alejandro's number. He picked up on the first ring.

"Hello, this is Alejandro speaking." The voice was formal, intense, masculine.

"Hey, it's Logan."

"*Logan!* Darling! I can hear by the background that you are on the fair isle of Manhattan."

"That I am. Heading to the interview at J/MA."

"Ah, with Chris. He's a good guy, that one."

"Thank you again for the lead."

"I just opened the door. It's up to you to walk through it."

"Right. Maybe we can do lunch after? You, me, and Franklin?"

"Well, that would be just lovely. I know the most fabulous place I've been wanting to try."

"Great. More soon then."

"Good luck, *mon cheri!*"

J/MA was between Eighth and Ninth Avenues and only a ten-minute stroll from Penn Station. The company had a surprisingly casual entrance, so low-key that I almost walked past it. I entered a lobby with dozens of awards mounted on the walls and dozens more in bookshelves around the room. Two secretaries faced one another across a large waiting room that looked like it was out of a fifties commercial: a red leather couch, black bucket swivel chairs, lamps that looked like metallic trees, and a glass table strewn with dozens of industry magazines. The size and energy of the room gave me a sense of the volume of people who came through in a single day. I looked at the two secretaries, unsure where I was supposed to go, until one finally looked up. She had dyed black hair, horn-rimmed glasses, and skulls tattooed up her left arm.

"Help you?" she asked.

"Stevenson," I said, my mouth dry. "Chris Stevenson?"

"Expecting you?"

"I hope so."

She winked at me. "'K, doll. I'll let him know you're here," she said. "Take a seat. You need some water or anything?"

"No thanks." I sat down on the red couch with a creak of leather. A few groups came through the door over the next five minutes, mostly young professionals not much older than me but decidedly more urban and sophisticated. Stylish haircuts. Pointy shoes. Flared collars. Black overcoats. Tattoos and more tattoos. When growing up in the shadow cast by my parents' own working-class childhoods, tattoos were seen as things reserved for bikers, prisoners, and others who had failed to rise above the challenges of their class. Sitting there, it was obvious that, at some point when I hadn't been paying attention, tattoos had made the jump from blue-collar to bourgeois.

A trim man stepped through a door. He had short-cropped brown hair and wore a tailored sky blue shirt tucked into tight jeans. A craggy nose overwhelmed his soft chin and his cheeks were pocked with acne scars.

"Logan?" When I stood, he extended a hand.

"Chris. Chris Stevenson." His handshake was firm, dry, professional. "Come on back," he said, opening the door and ushering me behind the creative curtain of the agency. We were in a hallway with offices on either side, more awards hanging in a seemingly endless parade, for typeface, most creative ad, best interactive design, most original campaign, best movie trailer, and on and on.

The hall gave way to an enormous common area that was, in essence, a blacked-out warehouse. Everyone seemed young and well dressed. I caught a ping-pong table in one area, a basketball hoop down a hallway, two foosball tables, and a pool table. There was a general buzz of conversation, typing at computers, and high energy.

'You guys survived the dotcom implosion," I noted.

"Helps when you're the best one out there. But the downturn still left its mark. We're three-quarters the size we once were. How was the trip up?" Chris walked behind me.

"Great. Train is civilized."

"A dignified way to travel," agreed the voice. "Up ahead to the right. Second door."

I stepped into an office not much bigger than a broom closet. There was a long window six inches wide and two feet long. Two chairs faced a narrow desk with barely enough room to squeeze behind. The room couldn't have been more than sixty square feet. Various posters, art, and action figures were spread about and there was a framed picture on the desk of Chris with his arms around what looked like either a boyfriend or a very close friend.

He pulled out my resume and indicated for me to sit. The single sheet of paper sat between us, alone on the very tidy desk. Four pens — one red, one black, one blue, and one green — rested in a square penholder. A dozen paperclips were in a plastic bin. A typewriter sat on a shelf to his left alongside an antique-looking stapler. When he spoke, his tone was soft but firm.

"So Logan, you're interested in working for us." A professional pause. Although not handsome, Chris was graceful, his features animated in a way that made his face intriguing and, after a few moments, elegant.

"I am."

"Great. Alejandro recommended you very highly." He paused, glancing down at the resume. "The job is to write the content for *Bed Bath & Beyond*. Do you know the company?"

"Sure. One of the big box stores. I've been in a couple."

A curt smile. "Great. And while I agree they're a box store, we want to avoid that description in these offices." He raised an eyebrow. "Clients are often lurking about."

"Got it."

"So they're ready to get on the Web — "

"*On* the Web?"

A headshake. "Yes. They're not yet, which is hard to believe, so we're building their website. It's scheduled to go live seven weeks from today, and we don't miss deadlines here. Which means we need all the content generated for that website, including descriptions for five thousand items."

I nodded.

"That's seven hundred descriptions a week, just to be clear."

I nodded again.

"Plus the photography of every single item. From multiple points of view. Plus a robust checkout system, inventory system, security, design." He paused to let that sink in. "So five thousand items photographed, tagged appropriately for searches, and described from scratch. My job is creative director for content. That means the content falls onto my shoulders, and I'm tasked with hiring three writers to do this job for me. I've found the other two already; I have a few people like you I'm considering for filling the final post." Chris paused. "This is a high-stress, high-deliverable, high-functioning environment. We do what we say we'll do, when we say we'll do it. You'd be tasked with writing one-third of the descriptions, or about two hundred twenty-five a week, give or take a few dozen." Another pause. "The other writers are all professionals. You're something else. Do you feel like this is something you could or would want to do?"

"Absolutely," I said. "I would really appreciate the opportunity, and I can write pretty much anything. As you can see from my resume, I've written a novel and I've done freelance work for companies in Philadelphia and Delaware."

Chris noted the resume with a glance. "Yes, I see that. I didn't read your novel, but I do remember a few friends of mine did and liked it very much."

He seemed torn for a moment, and I imagined him wanting to digress into a conversation about literature and the creative process. Instead he let out a breath of air. "This is the Web, and it's different. Different from a novel, of course, but also different from the print ads and print work you've done. The other writers are all print writers, so they need to learn on the fly, same as you. I'll need you to educate yourself on how to write for the Web — I'll send you some information you can read that will help."

I nodded, uncertain whether that meant I'd just been hired or not.

KEITH MARTIN-SMITH

"You can search AltaVista or Yahoo for *Bed Bath & Beyond* to see what comes up now. It's not generally pretty. So we'll also need you to write with search engines in mind."

Another nod.

"Do you know what that means?"

I cleared my throat. "No."

"I'll send those docs as well. You like to write?"

"I love it."

"So you'll get to write us a short story every day. Very, very short and very postmodern."

I laughed.

"And mostly about dishes and window treatments and five-hundred-thread count sheets, with some side drama involving toaster ovens and dough mixers."

Instead of laughing at his own joke, Chris sighed for a second time and leaned back in his chair, putting his hands across his belly. He glanced at the ceiling.

"I need to be honest with you," he said. "The only reason I agreed to this interview was on the strength of Alejandro's recommendation."

I nodded. "I understand."

"To be honest, I wasn't sure I was going to hire you before you walked into this office, but I'm liking what I'm seeing. You're curious and obviously smart. Two things we value."

I wondered at this assessment, since I'd said virtually nothing to prove I was capable of anything but the most basic of answers.

"I think you'll do a good job," he continued in a way that sounded like he was convincing himself. "So I'm going to take a risk on you. I'm a fair, good guy to work for. I'll warn you if you're not meeting my expectations, but I have to be clear: I don't have time to handhold or give you more than one warning. Are we clear on that?"

"Much clearer than a postmodern novel."

He grinned, nodding. "Now, as far as compensation: I can only free up four hundred a day for you. It's not much, I realize, but that's the highest we can go." Chris spoke tightly, as if I might balk at making nearly half my current month's salary in a single day.

I nodded, a little dumbly.

He stood and offered his hand. I stood and took it.

"I'll take you over to HR. They'll need all your personal info — address, social, and all of that. We'll compensate you for your train ride here and back today. And I'll introduce you to some of the team, give you a tour of this place, and then show you a place to work for the afternoon."

"Thank you, Chris. Really, thank you for taking a chance on me. I won't disappoint. I'll just need to make a phone call before we start. Need to change my lunch plans to dinner ones."

He stepped into the hall. "Use my phone. I'll be out here when you're done." He closed the door and I called Franklin.

"May I suggest the roast pork this evening? We had a taste of it earlier; it's quite sinful. It's been marinating for two days in a mixture of rosemary, mustard seeds, a fine white wine, and a blend of our chef's proprietary spices." The waiter's head was freshly shaved and his eyes a cool blue. He had the detached, intelligent air of someone putting himself through graduate school in something heady like philosophy or linguistics.

"May I suggest you get me another cocktail before I make a scene?" Alejandro replied. "Then we'll see about the pigs."

"Of course, sir. Same thing, or looking to mix it up a little?"

"He's mixed up enough," Franklin replied.

"Oh, just because you're straight, don't accuse me of being bent."

"The great Gatsby called; he wants his fedora back."

"*Ppht.* Gatsby was a pretender. I'm the real deal. You know," Alejandro said, shifting his attention to the waiter, "you have remarkable eyes."

"Thank you, sir." The waiter's detached politeness didn't waver.

"Your ass is great too."

The waiter's expression still didn't change. "Thank you again, sir." He paused. "Pilates."

"Oh, Alejandro, leave him alone. Do you make mocktails?" Lily asked.

"We can make any number of non-alcoholic drinks. What kind of taste were you looking for, ma'am? Something sweet? Something sour?"

"I think something that tastes like a gin and tonic," she said.

"You know what would taste just like a gin and tonic?" Alejandro asked. "Gin. And tonic."

"Cute," Lily said.

"Yes ma'am."

"Please don't call me ma'am. It makes me feel old."

"Yes miss."

"Or miss. That makes me feel pandered to."

The waiter looked momentarily stumped, but then said, "Well, just *yes* then. Our bartender will come up with something very tasty for you." He looked at Alejandro. "Without the gin. And without any misses or ma'ams."

"Two more scotches for us," Franklin said, leaning his head toward me.

"So," I said, raising my glass, "to Alejandro, for putting his neck on the line for me and landing me a great job."

We clinked glasses.

"Oh, happy to do it. If no one had helped me out, I'd still be serving breakfast at a shitty West Side diner."

"How long is the gig?" Franklin asked.

"He didn't say, but I'm guessing six or eight weeks."

"Congratulations, Logan." Lily said.

"Thanks."

"So," Alejandro said, "this is the gig to get you through to the next book."

"It and others like it. That's the idea. Did you read the draft I sent you?"

"Let's talk about it after dinner," he said.

I raised my eyebrows but didn't respond. A few minutes later, our waiter returned with our drinks.

"Here we have something fabulous for the fabulous one," he quipped, setting down Alejandro's drink. "Mocktail for the youthful yet empowered lady. And scotches for the twins. Now, would you all care to order or would you like more time?"

"A little more time," Alejandro said, not looking at him. "So: Los Angeles?"

Franklin nodded. "I think so."

"I think *not*," Lily replied.

He glanced at her and continued. "I've been in this city since 1987. I've been busting my ass here for a long time and I just can't get the kind of traction I want. I think LA will be more receptive to my style of art. New market, new audience."

"Better weather," Alejandro offered.

"For sure."

"It's a vapid, cultureless hole," Lily said. "I've always hated LA. Rude people, horrible traffic, smog, and an anti-intellectual streak a mile wide."

"Like I said," Franklin smiled, "more receptive to my style of work."

Alejandro and I laughed.

"How will you two manage?" I asked.

"Not sure yet," Franklin said, looking over to Lily. "But I've got to do something. This city, I mean, it's like I went out last night, right? I ended up in this kitschy bar on the Upper West Side, and it was full of all these fuckers wearing khakis and polo button downs. It was all the kinds of douchebags I moved to New York to get away from."

Alejandro laughed. "The fun with them is in the corruption. Most have never played with a man, but it's awfully easy to get those khakis off after a few drinks."

Lily shook her head at Alejandro. "You're truly incorrigible," she said, then turned to me. "We haven't figured it out," she said with an edge in her voice. "I would never stand in the way of your brother following his path but, the truth is, I'm not sure if LA is a place I can follow."

"We might have to do the long-distance thing," Franklin said without much conviction. "Or who knows? If I move it might suck and I'll come back to the city in a year."

"How's work going for you, Lily?" I asked.

She took a sip of her mocktail. "Great. Yoga is taking off everywhere. I have more work than I can handle and more offers to teach than I can take. Giving privates has been picking up, and there are a lot of people in this city who are willing to pay for one-on-one yoga instruction."

Alejandro opened his mouth to speak but closed it when he saw Franklin give a terse, single shake of his head.

"Good for you," I said. "You've made a real business out of something you love." I looked around the table. "That's not something anyone else here has managed to do."

"I do too many things," Alejandro sighed. "Franklin, maybe you can help me pare down. The photography, the illustration, the fine art. I can never settle on one thing." A cell phone chirped, and Alejandro put up an index finger, pulling out a tiny flip phone with his free hand. "Michelangelo, *darling*. So good to hear your voice. I'm supping with friends. Can I call you back in an hour? *Fabulous*." He snapped the phone shut and it vanished into his sport coat.

"You don't necessarily need to settle," Franklin said. "Just go deep into whatever you're doing. You can master more than one medium if you focus on them."

Alejandro waved a hand. "Focus. That's what I need more of. What's your secret?"

"Not wanting to live the alternative."

"Real job?"

"Real, non-teaching job. Nine-to-five commuter. Giving up on the dream."

Alejandro's eyes lingered on my brother before moving back to Lily. "So you're really doing that well with yoga?" he asked.

She nodded.

"Any marketing or anything?"

"No; it's all word-of-mouth referrals."

He sighed. "I should have been a yogi." He was perfectly serious, which made Franklin and me both laugh.

"There are lots of obvious reasons you couldn't teach yoga," said Franklin.

Pretend indignation. "Like what?"

"You'd be in jail for groping."

"Oh."

Our food arrived, shifting the conversation as we ate the two courses and had another few rounds of drinks.

Lily pushed back from the table. "I need to go. I have an early day tomorrow, and I know what happens when these two get together." She indicated Franklin and Alejandro.

"Fabulous, fantastic things?" Alejandro asked innocently.

"Through the lens of vodka, I'm sure that's how it seems."

"No," Alejandro countered. "Fabulousness is a state of being unperturbed by influence of spirits."

Lily ignored him and kissed me on the check as I stood to embrace her. "Congratulations again, Logan, on the job."

"Thank you. I hope to see you again soon."

"Darling," Alejandro said, offering his hand, fingers down. Lily took it. "You may kiss it if you wish," he said.

"Oh, fuck you, Alejandro," she said, squeezing his hand.

"Ow! Careful! I'm delicate!"

"As a boot."

"As a flower!"

"I'll walk you out," Franklin said.

Alejandro took a sip of his drink.

"So," I said, "the novel."

"Ah yes. The novel," he replied, looking at me as if over the tops of reading glasses.

"You don't like it." I hoped that wasn't the case, but it seemed the safest place to start.

He considered. "It's not that I don't like it. It's just … " He paused. "Look, I need to be direct. I can't stand beating around the bush."

I said nothing.

"Or," he said, "we can have this conversation more slowly. Have a little foreplay. It makes everything go down much easier."

I shook my head. "Give me the headline."

"Okay," he sighed. "The parts are all there. Good story. Well defined characters. Nice plot arc. Strong writing. It's all there, so it's hard to describe."

"I think you know how to describe it but don't want to tell me."

He nodded. "Fair enough. It's like the book doesn't have a soul."

"I don't follow."

"There's no élan vital, no *zeste pour la vie*," he gestured with his right hand. "Your last book was imperfect but it was *passionate*. This is like a mirror-opposite. It's a better book as far as plot and character creation, but it's dead inside."

When I still didn't reply, he spoke again. "Let's talk tomorrow. There are some really good things about it too."

I nodded.

"Oh honey, don't be so sensitive. Art is hard work. If it weren't, we'd all be successful at it. Which reminds me: you called me from a pay phone today?"

"Yes."

"They're called cellular phones. They're far more civilized than vomit-covered plastic toys reeking of the city."

"I don't need one."

He gave a little laugh. "I assure you, you do. Trust me. If you're going to work for one the cutting-edge ad agencies in Manhattan, and therefore the world, they're going to expect to be able to get hold of you someplace aside from your phone in *Philadelphia*." He paused.

"Yeah," I conceded, "you're probably right."

"Once you have one, you'll never know how you lived without it. In other news, are you dating?"

"Dating?" I was distracted, thinking about what he'd said about the book.

"Are you putting your penis into a woman's vagina on a regular basis, currently? Or a man's ass for that matter?"

I had to laugh. "No. On both fronts."

"Any particular reason you're not, aside from being hopelessly behind the technological times?"

"I dunno. I just haven't found anyone who's a good fit."

Alejandro took off his hat, setting it upside-down on the table. "Sex at all?"

"A few short flings here and there."

"I see." He considered. "I couldn't do it. How long has it been since that business with Carissa?"

"Six years, two months," I said, not having to pause to do the math.

"Long time," he mused, looking across the restaurant. "Long time. So sad. And you've been pretty much single ever since?"

"Are you saying the two are related? The deadness in the book and the lack of me being in relationship?"

He looked taken aback. "Oh honey! I certainly didn't say *that*. I'm not saying anything. You of all people should know I can't go more than a few sentences without thinking about sex."

I laughed.

"But," he said, staring at me with intense brown eyes, "now that you mention it, maybe you're right. Good art is born of pain and passion. You've had your share of the pain. Might be time to find the passion."

Philadelphia, 2004

Watch out for the poison ivy," Sylvie warned, glancing back. Her fine blonde hair, falling between her shoulders, moved easily with the twist of her head. She wore only a grey tank top and camouflage pants.

"On it," I replied. "Where is this place?"

"Oh, it's a bit farther."

Her body was waifish and, from the rear, it looked as if I might encircle her waist with just my two hands. She had moved to the U.S. with her family as a teenager, escaping communism in Poland and, while her English was flawless, an Eastern European accent marked her inflections. We had met six months earlier on an online dating site and had quickly fallen for each other. But I wasn't sure we were going to survive the near-constant turbulence between us.

There was a secret watering hole somewhere in Maryland she knew about. It was one of the things that made her so interesting; she was always exploring and finding strange, out-of-the-way places and things, from isolated watering holes to great undiscovered bands.

"What's going on with school?" I asked. "How was your last paper received?"

She ducked under a branch. "I haven't turned it in yet," she responded, without turning.

"I thought you were done."

"I am a woman with child putting herself through school and working in a pizza parlor. I do not have the luxury of time and energy that others have. I do the best I can. I asked for an extension. We'll see if they grant one."

She was twenty-six, with a five-year-old at home who sometimes stayed with her mother or her sister, as he was now. The father was living in Seattle, or Portland, or somewhere so far away as to be invisible. Sylvie was trying to finish her undergraduate work. She held onto the idea that getting her degree, and then a graduate-level one, would remove her from the indignities of her current existence. I was less sure, for I knew my fair share of baristas and barbacks with post-graduate educations toiling alongside their less educated peers.

"And you? You are happy with your novel?" The question floated back to me in the summer afternoon air.

"I dunno." I'd taken Alejandro's feedback to heart, not only to set about reworking the book but also finding a relationship. "It all seems so complicated. I guess I just want things to be simple." I wasn't sure if I was speaking about the book, the relationship I was now in with her, or both.

She slowed down as the path widened enough for us to walk side by side. We soon came to a creek and walked along the bank. "I am complicated and uncompromising," she stated, making me turn to her in curiosity. "I want unconditionally yet acknowledge that everyday conditions exist. We are all of us living compromised lives. You more than most."

She often spoke in this kind of lyrical, philosophical way that would make me take a long moment to consider what she'd just said, and if a little insult had been buried underneath her musings, as here, a moment or two more. I imagined her odd way of speaking was because of English being her second language, but for all I knew it was a reflection the strange corridors her thoughts traveled and the questionable conclusions she often reached.

"I suppose I'm less compromised than most," I began, attempting to respond to what she had said. "Still learning to define myself."

"Defining yourself even as you're bound to another."

"Bound to another? I don't follow." But she just looked straight ahead and smiled into the woods, walking faster. Her chin was round and cheekbones raised to either side of oversized blue eyes, and I often thought she would have looked very much at home on the cover of a fashion magazine; tall and exotic and somehow more than human.

"We're close," she breathed. We went around a ninety-degree turn in the creek, which then opened into a wide, lagoon-like area, twenty feet across. The woods were dense and the early afternoon warm and moist. She peeled off her shirt, exposing full breasts, kicked the sandals away, and pulled her pants off all in just a few motions. With a backward glance she jumped off the muddy bank, feet kicking up a clod of mud as she went.

"Holy shit!" I called, running up to see her naked and pale, treading water. She was laughing. "Jesus! How deep is it?" She pinched her nose and vanished, the blonde hair floating temporarily before being pulled into the darkness. A moment later she erupted out of the water to the waist, nipples pointing.

"*Deep!*" she breathed with a laugh, treading water again. "Come in — it's delightfully warm!"

I stripped slowly and self-consciously and stood for a moment on the bank, covering my genitals under her watchful blue eyes. I jumped. The water was so cold that I screamed as my head went under. Choking and sputtering, I managed to stutter "Holy fuck, it's *cold!*" But she was already laughing. She swam up and I grabbed her. I swam with her until my feet touched the rocky bottom, then lifted her naked onto the bank of the creek where I went down on her. She rubbed mud into my hair and planted her feet on my shoulders, leaning back into a shuddering and fast orgasm. When I entered her there was brown mud across the plain of her belly, and her blue eyes looked back at me with love and tenderness. Afterwards, shivering, we dove back into the water and then, finally frozen through, climbed back out and stood in a sea of goosebumps as we dried off. The sun was coming through an opening in the tree cover not far away as we wandered over, hand in hand, and sat on the grass in the sunlight.

"It's not that I need you to give up what you had," she said, as if we were in the middle of a conversation, her skin so white as to be nearly blue. "I just need you to accept what is. I am not like anyone else. Neither was she. No one is a duplicate."

I nodded, feeling very close to her. "She?"

"Carissa, of course."

"I appreciate the things you see," I said. "You're truly unlike anyone I've ever known." I smiled. "Unusual, but also smart. Passionate."

"I am none of those things. I am like you." She let go of my hand. "Just like you: a coward."

We sat together, me looking at her and her looking out into the woods, the sun falling all around.

"What the fuck are you talking about?" I said at last, fighting back my temper.

"My cowardice is because I fear I've destroyed myself to have a child, yet my love of him is so vast it's beyond anything I can put words to." She then said something in Polish, something I knew was more precise for her. "Yours is because you're focused so much on yourself; on what you've lost."

I shook my head. "I don't even know where to begin my argument with you." I gave her a dismissive laugh.

"Do you remember the first time we made love in your house in Philadelphia?" She didn't wait for me to answer. "I came into your office, afterwards, and you were there naked and looking at that photo of her. That one you keep on your desk. Your face: I think of your face then. I can see it now, can see the expression there, blown open in the way that only love can do — no secrets, no hidden vulnerability, no stories. Just naked. Really naked. I think about your face then and how when you turned to look at me you hid all those things back inside of yourself. And it felt like a blade."

"Oh come on. That's ridiculous. I was blown open from my time with *you*. Seeing Carissa's picture just brought it home to me. And you *surprised* me."

"The writer and his *words*," she sighed, shaking her head. She didn't argue points she felt were too obvious to reengage, I knew. "You're not a mother, but you understand love — you understand love as *wanting to be with*. And in that moment, yes, you and me and even her were all the same." She looked over at me with those terrifically blue eyes. "Your love for me is false."

I was stunned and enraged. "That's bold," I stammered. "The ways we've connected, the things we've said to each other." My heart was pounding. "The plans we've made — "

But she shook her head, interrupting. "Your heart is with *her*. It's not open to me. I keep waiting for it, and yes, you give it to me in small doses, like a drug, titrated over the sixty miles that separate us." Anger now in her tone. "You *are* dreadfully in love — that we share — but not with me. You've spent a lot of time trying to defend yourself from it, but it hasn't worked."

"That's absurd. Seriously, stop it. This is fucking crazy. I've — we've — I mean — "

"Stop what?" She let out a dismissive breath. "Telling the *truth*? Can you even tell me what it means to be in love?" Softness now; the velvet side of her.

"I — "

"You think you know what you're doing but you don't, and that makes you dangerous. Tell me. Love, Logan. What is it? Can you tell me?"

"That's hardly a question to — that's like — I mean," I felt trapped and was trying to find a way out, a way to get back on top of the conversation, the accusations. "That's like 'what's god' or 'what's truth' or something. What is love? It's just a feeling you have, a sense of rightness. A sense of belonging."

A laugh. "That's friendship, or coming home to your dog. Here, I'll make it easy for you: think of Carissa."

I flushed more deeply, in embarrassment and in rage. I wanted to slap her. And I hated Sylvie for daring to utter Carissa's name like that.

"It's *everything*," she continued. "That's a non-answer that's better than most. As my son has been my everything since he was born. That's what I want to be to you."

"Everything," I repeated as if trying the word out for the first time, knowing full well its impossibility, confused and furious and hopeful all at once.

"*Everything.*"

The sun was bright overhead and the sky the same intense blue as her eyes. I felt pushed in from all sides by brightness and blueness and intensity.

She spoke. "You've made me your hostage."

"So you're my victim?"

"A statement of fact. I'm hostage to you." Anger again. "You've made me hostage to hope; hope that your heart will heal and make room for me. We're just fucking, something to pass the time until the next one comes along. I want more than that! Fuck. I deserve more than that!"

"I don't understand," I said, almost pleading. "I don't know what you're talking about!"

The pupils of her eyes had dilated, great black holes spreading out from the center of the iris, swallowing all of the blue in their wake. She leaned in. "You hid that from me. Fuck. Maybe you hide that from yourself." She got up and walked away, her long toes twisting into the soft earth with each step. She put her tank top on, the nipples standing against its tightness. From the back I could see her wet hair clinging to her back and the goosebumps on her legs before her pants went over them. And with a feeling of anger I felt my desire for her, thick and strong and clear, the way it always was when we fought.

"Goddamn it," I muttered, standing. I walked up next to her with my cock rising, but she turned and went back to the sunny spot we had just left and sat down again. I began to follow her there and stopped, then went back and put my clothes on before rejoining her.

"I love you," I said, miserably, sitting down. "I'm doing the best I can."

"You're stuck," she replied, gentle once more. "And in being stuck you make me a hostage to hope. And I'll go on being hostage to hope if we stay together. With you, there's no room for an other. She owns your every moment."

"Sylvie," I said, moving onto my knees, "please stop. Please don't end this on some half-baked idea. I love you."

"Love," she said as if entranced, her voice distant and deep. "I have to steel myself against you. Even now, sitting here, I want you to convince me, as you have so many times before, that you really do love me."

"Come on. I *do* really love you."

"What do I see in you? Only everything, even when the love is so much more mine than yours. Even when I see with my own eyes what I'm denied. Even in my most realistic moments, like now. But I still can't help myself. I'm bound, really bound. Except to pull away. It's the only choice I have."

"I want to be with you, Sylvie. Yes, sometimes I have doubts. I have doubts, okay? Adam and Eve in the presence of the perfect being, their maker, were still drawn to other possibilities, to alternatives, to *doubt*."

Only a tiny corona of blue remained in each eye; I feared they might go entirely black.

"They were drawn to *hope*, Logan, not driven by doubt."

"Sylvie — "

"It's okay." Tears ran down her cheeks. " I see it now. Such clarity." Her eyes flickered upwards to the sky. "It is not inconsistent to have loved me insanely and still wanted to preserve an escape vent. How could you not, given what happened to you? You paid such a terrible price for your surrender. I wanted to lick your wounds the way you've licked mine. You have so many." She put her hand on my arm, and I was shocked at how warm she was. "But she owns your every moment."

She stood and wiped her legs and glanced down at me: time to go. I stood and we walked silently together through the woods, the entire half hour back to the car, without uttering a word. Once inside her car and heading back to her apartment, she spoke.

"You can get a shower at my place if you'd like."

"I would like that. Thank you."

Another forty-five minutes in silence, and then we were in her small, cramped apartment. I went into her bathroom and turned the shower on nearly as hot as it would go, closing my eyes to the blast of scalding water. A moment later I felt cold hands on the sides of my belly, and opened my eyes to see Sylvie there. She kissed me with a profound gentleness and I leaned her back against the tiles. Lifting her legs around my waist, I entered her as she clung to me.

Philadelphia, 2005

A mostly empty bottle of red wine stood in front of me. I was sitting at the vintage table that had come from my grandmother's home. It was of modest size, taking up only a small part of my living room. With its four matching dark wood chairs with red cushions sewn into them, it gave the impression of a fine antique, although if you looked carefully you could see where a thin cherry veneer had been glued over pine on the upward-facing side of the table, making it worth a couple of hundred bucks instead of a couple of thousand. A poor man's antique. Two candles burned over a notebook. On the pages, my particular blockish writing, messy and largely illegible to any eyes but my own, looked up at me.

Sylvie and I had lasted barely two months from that day in the park. She had ended things more definitely and less dramatically on a rainy August evening over the phone, with grace and clarity. I had argued with her for a short time but then relented: there is no wisdom in convincing someone to take you back, for that was merely postponing the inevitable day when the ax will fall again, very likely with less kindness. I missed her intensity and strange, elliptical way of thinking and speaking, her confidence and power, and the sex. As to the merits of her arguments, I wasn't yet sure. She was such a mess herself that it was hard to tell where her baggage ended and mine began.

That had been a year ago. Now, with the additional free time of bachelorhood, I had thrown myself into reworking the novel. I had pushed Sylvie and Carissa and New York and just about everything else out of my mind and focused on making the book deeper, better, grander in its scope and ambition. In my near-complete isolation, I was sure I was writing a masterpiece. My days and nights had been spent typing into my iBook, either for my freelance clients or for myself. Yet when I submitted the novel to Rebecca at Random House, it was turned down with a polite but uninformative letter. I'd tried another half dozen publishers with the same result.

Still, I believed in the work and was confident I could self-publish the book and, using my contacts and lists, sell some copies through my own website, create a splash, and find a publisher by demonstrating the success of the self-published version. It had been expensive to do, and six months had passed since I'd received my two boxes of books.

I let my eyes travel across the narrow space, at once a living and dining room, and into the kitchen at the back of the house. I stood up, taking the wine with me, and wandered around the dimly lit downstairs. The radiators were gurgling softly. I walked into the kitchen and leaned against a counter. Across from me was a green and white hutch filled with wine glasses. It had a glass front and I had strung Christmas lights through the back of it.

I looked out the back door and into the tiny yard, now covered in snow. In the mudroom, just beyond the door, sat the two boxes containing the remaining three hundred or so copies of my novel. The boxes had moved with me once already, and I hadn't opened them to mail a sold copy in several months.

I stepped outside. It was late, probably close to one in the morning, and my breath condensed like an apparition. I listened to the traffic in the distance and looked west. West. I'd been on the East Coast the whole of my life. I wondered about moving, about starting over somewhere else. There wasn't much keeping me in Philadelphia except habit. I had a few friends I saw infrequently, some bar buddies, and Alejandro a few hours north, but nothing that felt uniquely mine. And Franklin had been in LA for nearly two years. While Philadelphia was now full of the familiarity of inherited geography, I wondered if home might be somewhere else.

I turned the bottom of the wine glass to the sky, went back into the mudroom, and looked at the two boxes full of thousands of dollars worth of books. With a grunt I stacked one on top of the other, then hauled them through the house and out the front door. I opened the recycling bin to reveal a ménage of *New York Times*, wine bottles, and junk mail, and then I poured the books out like water from a pitcher. I methodically broke down the box and slid it behind the books, newspapers, and bottles, then poured the second box's contents in. I closed the lid and went back inside.

Wednesday

I sit back from my computer, looking at the memories encoded in bits of data on the screen that have just tumbled out of my head and though my fingers with such speed my arms are aching. Some of these I'd nearly forgotten, especially the intensity of Sylvie. I look down the hall at the darkened doorway of the master bedroom.

I stand and stretch, check the time, and groan. It is nearing three; I've been writing for almost five hours without a break. After using the bathroom I decide to climb into the bed in my study and, for the first time in what seem like weeks, fall asleep immediately.

I'm groggy when I awaken, but a few cups of coffee and NPR on the drive help get my brain moving. I decide, for now, not to think about what's happening in my life. I have my job; I need to work it long enough to get out of debt, get my head straight, find out what's missing at home, and get back on track.

Steve isn't at work when I arrive. Jen and Jamie have their heads down as I make my way to my desk. Neither looks up at me, which is a little odd, but it's a busy company so I settle into my day without giving it another thought. I've crushed it this week. Everything that's been asked of me I've managed to get done, and I feel satisfied. I'm busy working on some longer term projects I can do for the company when Steve comes in an hour later. He doesn't look at me as he approaches his desk, and I notice his face is red and distracted. He puts his bag down and pulls out his cell phone, then walks back toward the doors while making a call. After ten minutes he hangs up the phone, still red-faced and looking resigned. I stare at my computer and watch him approach in my peripheral vision.

"Hey," he says and I feign surprise.

"Oh, hey."

"See you in Square?"

"Sure."

"Now?"

"Sure."

Square is, not surprisingly, the smaller cousin of Rectangle and is used for less formal meetings.

"Gimme a moment to get my things." I sound extra cheerful, even optimistic, like we're about to discuss the size of our bonuses. I linger longer than I intend but finally get a notebook and a pen. I can't help but notice that Jen and Jamie still have not looked up at me. Jamie is curling a long strand of her dark hair around her right index finger, chewing gum in a way that brings her jawline into magnificent relief with each bite.

I go around our desks and into the hallway closest to me, the one that takes you upstairs to the army of developers who work in black-walled seclusion. I push the door open into Square and am shocked to see the HR woman, Nancy, facing me. Her expression is dour but professional, hands clasped neatly together on top of a large folder.

I stutter at the entrance.

Steve is facing partially away from me with a tiny notebook and a pen in front of him. Patches of red still remain on his face. He glances briefly at me.

"So have a seat," he says.

The room is tiny, about a hundred and fifty square feet, with functional Berber carpet beneath a white conference table. It's too brightly lit, its only window looking back out on the darkened hallway I just exited.

"So," Steve says, his eyes finally rising to meet mine, "you know, things just aren't working out and we're going to have to make this your final day with us, effective immediately. We're going to pay you for the rest of the month. But it just hasn't been a good fit. Nancy will explain everything else."

I look down at my notebook and pen. Steve stands awkwardly, pauses as if he can't remember what else he planned to say, and then exits without looking back.

"I'm sorry, Logan," Nancy says immediately. She's a middle-aged woman with curly brown hair, a long nose, and dark circles under her eyes. Her straight teeth are yellowed, and her lips form a thin line when she's not speaking.

"These things happen," I say, stupidly, as if it's my job to comfort her.

Did I just get fired?

"So let's go through what happens next," Nancy begins, the thin lips pulled even more tightly into each other and turned downward in that universal sign of distress. She speaks with the all the deliberation of a sober woman speaking to a drunk, no doubt born of having had many of these conversations with people in the kind of shock that I'm currently experiencing. "Now. Everything I'm about to go over is in this folder." She pats the folder maternally, like it's a child's freshly washed head. "Every word, so you can review *everything* when you have a moment. And you can call me anytime to ask me to repeat anything we covered here, or email me, day or night. Is that clear, Logan?"

I nod.

She explains the terms of my termination: immediate, and that I will receive three weeks pay so long as I don't speak out publicly against the company, in social media or other places, for up to twelve months, otherwise they can rescind the payment.

"But you don't have to take the money," she adds, seemingly without any innate bias, "and then you can say whatever you like. It's really up to you."

"I'll take the money over a few snarky posts on Facebook."

She nods, looking at me as if I've just said something that, if not profound, is wise. I suddenly want to get out of there, but she goes on. More detail about my healthcare — terminated at the beginning of the next month, my stocks — returned to the company since I didn't finish one full year, and other sundry details that I don't recall. I sign a number of papers, which all get put into a briefcase sitting under the table. The recently patted folder slides across the table to me.

"This is yours."

I take it.

"Do you have any questions for me, Logan?"

"I think I'd just like to go home."

She nods. "Of course."

I emerge from the hallway into the grand office space, feeling like I am in a spotlight. No one is looking at me, but everyone seems to be noticing me. As I walk back to my desk, I see that both Jen and Jamie are gone. I look over my things and realize that I only want to make one trip. It's bad enough to have to walk out, having just been fired. But having to walk back in to get another armful of crap is simply not tolerable, so I make a cold calculation about what I'm willing to leave behind.

A few moments later I lift my bag, overflowing with items normally left behind at the end of a workday, and sling it heavily over my shoulder. Steve is sitting at his desk and, I imagine, pretending to work, but I stop anyway.

"Hey," I say, "no hard feelings. Business is business." I offer my hand and he takes it.

"Good luck, Logan."

I nod.

As I push through the doors and out into the parking lot, I feel the collective relief of the office now that this awkward moment, this reminder of corporate mortality, has vanished.

I've never been fired from a job, ever, not even my first few as an irresponsible teenager, so this is a new feeling in my body. I unlock my car door and sit on the cold leather seat. Under the surprising sense of freedom is something darker and less welcome, coiling in the belly, something rotten. *Fired*.

I start the car, pull out my phone, and remember that the previous night Alea had friend requested me. I open Facebook, accept the request, then immediately message her:

Hey

A moment later she responds.

Hey yourself. How you feeling after that massage?

It was unlike anything I've ever experienced. I'm still tingling.

Me too.

So this is kind of odd, but I just got fired from my job.

What? Seriously??

Yeah. It's all good.

The Muggles. You didn't belong with them.

What are you doing?

Nothing. Just getting moving if you really need to know. Got a few errands to run but free by two. You're on Ninth and Broadway?

Yup.

I'm just ten blocks away. Why don't you come by once I'm free?

The house is a modest downtown ranch of tan brick with a large stone porch. It's raining, and I make my way up her walkway with my head pulled inside the upturned collar of my coat, not wanting to rush in case she's looking out a window but also not loving the feeling of the freezing rain on my head. I pause outside the door, thinking about darting back to my car and away from the madness that might lie inside but, as I'm contemplating this sanity, the door opens and she's standing there, hair wild and free, green eyes peering out from that strong face.

"Are you going to just stand there?" she asks, opening the screen door.

"I was, in fact, thinking about it," I admit, as I step in. She's barefoot, so I take off my boots while leaning against the wall. Her red dress ends just above the knee, and the low cut in the front shows me there is no bra underneath. I take off my coat, unsling my computer bag, wondering why I'd brought it inside, and run a hand through my wet hair.

"So here you are," she says, taking a step closer, so close she's almost touching me. "Do you want to talk about what happened?"

"Getting fired?"

"Yeah."

I shrug. "I feel a little bit ashamed, but mostly I feel relieved."

She nods. "You're not really a company man."

"I suppose not."

"Can I share something with you?"

"Sure." We're still standing near the door.

"You've got a lot of complexity in there. Layers of it pass over you and through you and around you. The bits I can see. Others you keep more deeply locked away, but I get a sense of them."

I look into those eyes, almost a metallic green, ten thousand fractals inside her irises, then make a fast sweep of the house: an open floor space, a ragtag couch, a used kitchen table in the far corner, books and candles and stale incense, a few threadbare throw rugs over a hardwood floor, and a cavernous fireplace. When I look back to her, she's looking harder at me.

"That."

"What?"

"That. You take it all in. You watch. But you really *see*. It almost makes me nervous."

I suppress a smile. "Almost."

"But there's more. A longing. A loss. I felt it last night during your massage, something almost shameful, a wall. Desire. Needing to be met.

To join souls. You're disciplined, but beneath this man who has learned to control all his appetites, lies a very, very hungry person."

She cocks her head to one side. Looking down at the hardwood floor and away from her eyes, I see feet step closer to me, the long toes spreading out across the floor, and when I look up she's only inches away. Her lips part, and I grab her behind the neck and pull her into me, kissing her deeply, her hands up my shirt and onto my back in an instant, her skin cold against mine. I take her by the throat and push her across the den and pin her against the wall. I kiss her as deeply as I'm able, and then close my hand around her throat. Her face turns red.

"*Fuck* you," she breathes between kisses, shoving at me until I pin her arms with my hands, biting her neck. In one quick movement, I turn her around to press her body up against the wall, holding her head in place with a fistful of hair and her body with my own.

"Fuck *you*," she whispers, lifting her hips and pressing them out and into my body. With a free hand I pull her panties down and open my pants, and when I go inside of her she arches her back and pushes back from the wall.

"Fuck me harder. *Fuck you!* Fuck me *hard*! Come on!"

And I do, until sweat is dripping off the tip of my nose, and then we move from the wall to the floor, and from the floor to the couch, and then to a coffee table, and finally to her bedroom. When I finally cum it's into her waiting mouth, and she maintains direct and unabashed eye contact as the orgasm threatens to extinguish me, but this time I fight back and stay in the room, in my body, in my connection to her.

I collapse onto her chest, feeling the scratch marks forming on my back, the sting of her nails carving themselves, I imagine, into long red divots across the skin. I kiss her and then roll onto my back, and she curls around me like a feline.

Our breathing slows; she pulls a blanket onto us.

"That was amazing," she purrs.

"Yeah," I agree. "It's been a long time since I fucked like that. I wasn't sure I had it in me anymore."

"That," she says, "is a crime."

I don't respond. In some ways her room looks typical for someone in her twenties; a tapestry, some new-agey shit like dream catchers and crystals, but there's also her art — otherworldly and witchy, dark greens and purples and yellows and reds of swirling figures, animals, and landscapes.

"You're a fighter," she says, "who somehow got stuck behind a desk. This is your celebration of freedom."

I laugh a little. "I like your art."

"Thanks. I'll show you the studio before you leave. It's out back."

"You remind me of someone," I say, *fighter* sticking in my mind. "It's really in more ways than one."

"Who?"

"My ex-finance, from a lifetime ago."

"Oh?" Curiosity.

"She was amazing. Carissa. She was a lot like you, except shorter."

"Most people are — shorter," she notes, and I laugh. "So what happened?"

"Well," I say, "we'd gotten engaged and I'd gotten my first book published but it hadn't yet come out. It was a magical, amazing time."

"Your first book. I picked it up and started reading it after we met. It's excellent."

"Thanks," I say automatically, then take a moment to receive the compliment. "Feels like it was written by another person, but thank you."

"You were in love, your book was published — you were on the path," she says. "No Muggles anywhere in sight. So what happened?"

"Yeah," I say, "things just got complicated, the way they can in life."

She considers that, and waits, but there's no more. "Bullshit, Logan," she says, putting a hand between my legs and literally squeezing my balls.

"Ow!"

"Out with it. What's hiding in there? Are you so fucking mysterious on purpose, or does it just come naturally to you?"

I laugh. "Naturally."

"Seriously. What happened?"

"You really want to know?"

"I do."

I close my eyes. It takes me awhile to start to speak. "It's funny," I say, and of course it's not funny at all. "I've never really talked about it. Weird, really. One Friday night, you know? She went out with her friend, Amy. Amy and Carissa. Trouble, those two." I hear Alea's lips part in a smile. "And sometimes they'd get pretty bombed, so when I went to bed at two and she wasn't home, no big deal, you know? But I woke up the next morning — she slept at my place almost all the time — and she still wasn't home, and I got worried. I called Amy, and she said they'd parted ways at two fifteen or so the night before and that Carissa was heading over to my place. So I had to call her parents, my brother, the cops, you know? It's weird — you're so worried you can't even feel how worried you really are. Detectives showed up at my door that afternoon. New York City detectives. Like out of a bad TV show, two cops who were so fucking calloused you could have thrown them out of a moving car and not hurt them."

I open my eyes as Alea sits up, her left hand covering her breasts. I don't look at her but instead at a pair of sneakers on her floor, tumbled over each other, laces scattered.

"Detectives," I continue, "told me she was in the hospital, so I went. Her parents had made it up to the city at that point. But the look of the nurses and doctors told me she was fucked. Then I saw her. Little

Carissa. *My* little Carissa. Broken. Tubes and shit running out of her and bandages that covered most of her head. She was on a respirator, which is fucked up if you've ever seen one in person — a big, ugly plastic tube taped over her mouth and a machine breathing for her." My voice sounds like it's coming from another part of the room, a recording stretched across an old tape, the intonation and speed all wrong. "The bruises. Man, those bruises. Her face all swollen and this grey-blue color. Stitches, busted lips, broken nose. We get the story from the cops; she'd been mugged, beat with a tire iron, raped. They had the guy and got semen from the rape kit. He was some crackhead from Alphabet City who'd been in and out of Rikers. Fractured her skull, broke her jaw and nose and collarbone, and left her for dead. Blunt force trauma and all of that. Jogger found her in the morning, still breathing, but in a few hours she had stopped and had to be intubated. Needed surgery on the jaw but that was not as serious as the damage to her brain. Her parents decided to turn off the machine the next day, when the scans showed she was already gone, just a bruised shell. My book came out the next month and it did really well, which was weird because I didn't do any press or anything. Just moved to Philly."

I clear my throat. I'm looking at my own feet sticking out from under the blanket, falling away from each other on the bed, their December paleness making them look like white socks. I notice I need to clip my toenails, and then I realize Alea is still sitting and looking at me, one arm now clutching her breasts, the other one over her opened mouth. Tears are running down her cheeks, and her hair is the mane of a feral creature, wild and uncontained.

"Logan," she breathes through the hand. "I am so. Sorry."

I come more into the room and blink a few times, clearing my throat again. It's raining outside, the light of the day exhausted, and she and I are inside of long shadows.

"Oh," I say, sitting up. "Oh. It's okay."

She stares and shakes her head firmly. "No. No, it isn't. It isn't okay at all."

It's hard for me to move through the fog of my mind. "It was a long time ago."

"What the fuck difference does that make?" Her right hand has come away from her face, but the other one is still across her breasts.

I don't respond, but I do manage to sit up. "Do you have any tea?"

She looks confused. "What?"

"Tea."

"Uh, I think we might." She lets the hand fall away from her chest, and I see her small nipples hard against the cold. She slides off the bed and pulls a blue robe from the back of the door, wrapping it around her and padding out of the bedroom toward the kitchen. I rise, and realize I have to go into the front room to get dressed. My clothes, along with her red dress and panties, are in a tangled mass like fall leaves scattered out of a pile. I find a sock here, my shirt there, my boxer briefs inside my jeans. The clothes, wet, are cold against my skin and, by the time I walk back into the kitchen shivering, the kettle is rumbling.

"What kind of tea?" she asks.

"I don't care."

She looks at me strangely.

The kitchen is rustic, with brown linoleum underfoot, white cupboards with glass fronts, and a dark Formica counter. Plants hang from the corners, a large back window gives a view into the afternoon, the shadows now so heavy on the ground that it looks close to nightfall even though we've barely passed the middle of the day.

She pours two cups, taking hers in both hands in a way that makes me think of home, and I feel the bitter taste of shame. I pick up my cup and sip. Some kind of herbal blend. Alea is looking at me — staring, really — and I finally meet her green gaze.

"You're fucked up, do you know that?"

"I'm sorry?"

"You just told me about your finacée getting raped and beaten and murdered, and you didn't so much as sniffle. What the fuck is wrong with you?"

"I'm sorry?"

"Are you ears as broken as your heart? Don't you feel *anything*?" She looks wary, angry. Rage rises but I clamp my jaws across its back and instead of telling her to go fuck herself, I stare intently at the floor.

"Oh," she mocks, "*there's* some feeling. Well done. Careful, or you might *show* something."

I take a forced breath. "Sometimes," I start, but it's hard to speak with my jaw so tight. "I feel too much." I look up. "I just don't want to vomit my emotions onto you."

"So considerate of you. Really. Let's just not consider that you were just *inside of me*, or that you just *came in my mouth*." She throws one of her hands up. "I mean, *fuck*, Logan. You use your words, sure. But are you a fucking robot?"

"I'm sorry," I repeat defensively, not really sorry at all. "I don't like to talk about. It."

"*Of course* you don't like to talk about it." Her head tilts to one side. "I *know* it's fucking hard. How could it *not* be? How could it *not* be something you want to get as far fucking away from as you can?"

My rage morphs into a watery feeling in my gut that makes my knees weak. I fight to stand up straight but I have to lean onto the counter.

"Logan," Alea says, more softly now, setting her cup on the counter, "for fuck's sake." I accidentally drop my mug. "You're frozen in time. And dead inside until you let that shit through you."

"It would destroy me," I say so quietly I don't know if she hears me.

"No, sweetie. It would free you."

The moment passes. The feeling comes back into my legs. I see my overturned mug and the puddle of tea and detach myself from the support of the counter.

"Sorry about the tea."

"Fuck the tea."

"Well, let me wipe it up."

"Fuck the floor."

But I do, carefully, focusing completely on the task at hand. Alea leans against the counter, watching me through those green lenses. I get the sense that, if she knew me just a little bit better, she would slap me.

"I should probably get going," I say, putting the paper towel into the trash and my mug into the sink, avoiding her eyes.

She nods. Her arms are folded across her chest, the eyes never looking away.

"I'll be in touch."

She doesn't respond.

I walk through the neat Spartan living room and out the door, into the gloom of the gray day. I stand in the front yard, watching the rain and the water run down the grass and across the sidewalk. My head and the back of my neck quickly grow cold but I stand there a long time, until a violent shudder draws me back into time and place. I get into the car and notice the condensation on the windshield as I begin to realize it's all coming to an end, that my life has been beaten back onto itself and that when the sun comes up tomorrow, it will dawn on the ruin of me.

Wednesday Night

The drive home is the longest forty minutes of my life. I am in the middle of an explosion happening in slow motion, a microsecond lapse that lets me feel the impact of each quantum of time as it passes, taking pieces of me as it goes.

As I walk through the door, she's making dinner, pulling kale leaves carefully off their stalks.

"Hey stranger," she says, "how are you?"

"Hi," I reply, dumping my bag by the door and kicking off my shoes. I walk toward the kitchen. Her hands, slender and long and with the nails white at the tip, are massaging oil into the greens. She cuts some carrots and they follow the kale into the oven. On the table two candles burn. She bends over the stove for a moment. "You look awfully serious, mister," she says with a playful glance.

"Was just a long a day," I mumble.

She moves delicately, wiping a patch of countertop. For some reason I recall the time, years ago, when she organized a surprise birthday party for me, and how genuinely surprised I'd been at the friends who had come to celebrate me — and us. And how in love I'd been with her then, the dull ache I'd felt my chest whenever I looked over to her that night. I remember how that ache, that love, seemed capable of delivering us into greater happiness than either of us could generate for ourselves.

She puts the sponge in the sink and comes over to me. "Are you okay," she asks, putting a warm hand against my cheek. "Woah — you're burning up!"

"I'm fine. Just tired." I deflect. "What about you?" She takes her hand back and meanders, happily, into a description of her day, and I ask a few questions to keep her talking, watching her lips form the words, watching when something makes her smile, and once she lets out a little laugh that I'm afraid might make my knees go weak again. I smile too but I'm sure my eyes are hollow and false. I realize that, if she knew the truth, she would never look at me like this again, never act like this around me again. I consider simply pushing sex with Alea down into a deep hole of my being where it can't be seen, or felt, and just go through the motions of being in a loving, monogamous, and faithful relationship. In time, the memory would fade to a black and white image and it could be business as usual again. But then I think of Carissa. And Alea. And of what just happened. And how the images of Carissa have gained such power and strength over the last two weeks of writing about her. She now seems achingly real once more and unwilling to be kept inside the black box of willful forgetting.

I can come clean tomorrow, I think, *or after the weekend.* Just one more weekend to be together, to appreciate what is before it's all blown to shit. But I know, standing there and watching her, I know that I can't keep stuffing things down, that Alea was right: the only way out is through, and coming clean is the only path that makes any sense at all. Coming half clean, after all, still leaves you dirty.

"God," she is saying, opening the oven door to pluck a piece of the warm kale, "I can't believe it's almost Christmas! I'm so excited for the time off! We should take a trip." She's speaking quickly, the way she does when she's excited and forgets herself a little. "You've been working so hard. You have time off as needed, which means we could take a week right after the New Year to go somewhere nice, somewhere warm. Mexico? Hawaii? Someplace where we can connect again ... "

"Can we sit down?" I hear myself say. "I need to talk." I'm not certain what's about to come out. Maybe just how unhappy I am. Maybe just that I got fired. That would be enough. That would explain plenty and give me room to decide what I want to do, or to admit.

Her light mood folds into a vigilant crease that appears above her eyes, and she looks at me warily. "Of course."

She sits at the head of the table and I sit on her right. Her light blue wool sweater fits her slender frame, and her long hair spills across both shoulders. We look at each other. I see her mouth tighten against what might come.

"I got fired today," I say.

She blinks and looks straight ahead for a few breaths and steadies herself, as though she believes that if she controls her body and her voice she can control me, the room, what might come next. "What happened?"

"Steve called me into a conference room this morning and told me it wasn't working out. That was pretty much it." I imagine thoughts of our wedding going through her head, and the neatly planned life we were heading toward, now under threat.

"The stock?"

I shake my head.

"Severance?"

"More than they had to. Three weeks, as long as I don't criticize them on social media."

"Three weeks."

It's not enough to for us to take that vacation.

"Did you know?"

"No. I thought maybe a reprimand, maybe a warning for being a flaky artist-type, but not fired. There's no one to do my job." I pause, adding unnecessarily, "I've never been fired before."

"So what are you going to do?"

I shake my head. "I don't know." And then I'm saying the horrible, tearing thing that will cut through to her soul; the words of nightmares and betrayal, the unspeakable selfishness of me. "I had sex with someone else. Today. After work. After I got fired. A girl I met in a coffee shop a couple of days ago."

She goes completely still; even her chest ceases to move. The room goes still with her, and I'm pulled into the awful infinity of a moment that stretches out between us. She's staring straight ahead, her mouth opened slightly. Both of her hands are on the table, palms down, and her engagement ring is breaking the soft candlelight into fractals. With what looks like profound effort she turns her head toward me, the eyes swiveling from infinity and into the room, and then onto me.

"What?"

The word evaporates between us. I stare back.

"*What?*" she repeats and, in another heartbeat, her breath comes with a gasp, and with it veins onto on the sides of her forehead, lips pulled back, eyes wide and unblinking. Those downward-facing palms slam themselves onto the table as she shrieks something I don't understand and then she is standing and throwing her empty plate against the wall, the glass raining down around us.

"Who?"

"What?"

"*WHO?*"

"A woman I met at a coffee shop."

"Do you love her?"

"What?" That question makes no sense to me whatsoever.

"*Do you love her?*"

"I hardly know her!"

"What? Why? *Why? How could you?*"

I stand and step toward her with my arms outstretched but she steps back and her right arm goes up. I'm surprised when I realize I'm crying and unsure what I'm seeing until her hand slaps across my face, hitting so hard my head turns. I'm momentarily stunned, and find my eyes are on the candles whose flames wobble uncertainty. There's a sense of deep relief in the impact, in the pain, and I turn back to her with no answers, nothing to say that could possibly justify what I've done, no understanding of my own actions, wanting her — needing her — to keep hitting me.

"I'm sorry," I repeat, reaching out to touch her arm but she recoils with a face distorted in horror.

"Don't touch me!"

I freeze.

"Get out. *Now.*"

And in that moment some part of me screams to do just that: get out. And so I go upstairs to grab a handful of things, rushing now. As I step from the bathroom and into the hallway she's there, face torn open, eyes wide in their sockets, nothing left to lose. She shoves me into a wall, hard, and lands another slap as I drop to my knees, wanting her to hit until I no longer have to feel anything else, but she stops and stares with eyes that don't comprehend. "I'm sorry," I slur through snot and tears and the taste of blood. "I'm so sorry."

"Get out," she repeats, suddenly composed in a way that terrifies me.

And so I do, running down the stairs and grabbing my shoes without putting them on and out into the yard and into my car and hitting the gas even before the transmission has managed to settle into gear. The car lurches forward uncertainly and snaps my head against the headrest and I drive and drive and drive.

Thursday

I'm looking through my phone while sitting in the cavernous space, the white textile roof overhead making me think of the inside of a zeppelin. It's dry and hushed and every forty or so feet a column rises out of the ground to support the fabric above, pulled tight as a drum. Sounds come in murmurs or sudden clatters. Even though most of the storefronts are dark, everything is bright and hard.

I text her: *I am so sorry. I don't know why I blurted all that out, why I did what I did. I'm so sorry.*

I am prepared for anything, but what comes makes me stare: *I'm blocking you, here and on email, as well as Facebook and Instagram. Don't contact me. I'll have one of my friends contact you regarding details about the house and your belongings.*

I frantically type: *Oh come on. Please don't shut me out. I know I fucked up. Beyond fucked up. I know I destroyed us. Please don't do it this way. We can still talk, even if it's just about the logistics. I'm at the airport now. Am going to go spend some time with Franklin. Will be back in a few days.*

I hit send and waited. Nothing. I wait a minute. Two.

Hello?

Another minute.

Hello?

I call her but it goes straight to the message. I don't leave one. My phone is down to a quarter charge. I have only my wallet, my phone, and the clothes on my back. Supersaver airlines are the only ones flying to LA at this hour and I can't buy a ticket through my phone at the last minute, so I have to track down an open counter and purchase a fare the old-fashioned way. I have twenty-five minutes to get to the gate.

I hustle to security. An older businessman is waiting with a deflated sense of urgency, his suit crumpled from his mid-back to knee. In front of him is a girl in her twenties, furiously chewing gum, hair dyed black and razor-straight. She's barefoot even though it's freezing outside, her combat boots already in hand. She loads her belongings onto the conveyor belt and is beckoned past the wave-generating machine where you have to hold your hands up like you're being robbed. The businessman is a pro; shoes slide off, computer slips out and into the bin, and leather computer bag settles neatly behind the modest carry-on.

I have nothing to remove except my shoes, phone, and car keys. I step through and the dour-faced security guard stops me. She has a square jaw, dull eyes, and wears the evidence of a long-ago battle with acne on both cheeks, visible even under badly applied makeup.

"Where are your bags?"

"I don't have any."

"You check a bag? Sir?"

"No."

A suspicious look.

"Where are you going?"

"Los Angeles."

"For what purpose?"

"Family."

"Step to the side, sir." I look behind me. No one. A lanky man coiled on a chair stares at what must be my pair of shoes, phone, and car keys. I watch with envy as the businessman and the young girl walk away and disappear down the stairs.

"Come on," I plead.

"Over there, sir."

"For fuck's sake."

My remark warrants some mumble into a walkie-talkie, and with a sigh I step aside and wait. A tall man with olive skin and a belly that's putting tremendous pressure on the buttons of his uniform emerges. He proceeds to ask me the same questions. He has a luxurious mustache, black and full. I answer with as little sarcasm as I can muster. They inspect my phone, test my shoes for something. Look over my keychain. Take everything out of my wallet. Have me turn my pockets inside out. Give me a pat down just shy of an erotic massage. I am clearly on my way to a strip search by the mustachioed specimen when I speak up.

"Listen," I say, digging deep to find some humanness. "I have four minutes to get to my gate. I imagine that means I'm going to need to sprint, and even then it's going to be dicey. I know you're just doing your job and keeping everyone safe, and — " I have to swallow before I say this, "I appreciate that. But my relationship of five years ended tonight. Badly. With my fiancée. I have nowhere to sleep unless I get on that plane and fly out to see family. Please."

The man's eyes, a similar color as his skin, don't blink or show any emotion.

Fuck, I think. *Flight missed.*

He hands me my phone. "Better run," he says.

"Thanks," I breathe, snatching my shoes and keys and bolting down the stairs, sliding in my socks. There is a tram waiting and I jump onto it and in two minutes I'm out, shoes firmly laced, taking stairs two at a time and then running down a long corridor. I can see the gate and a flight attendant's bleached blonde hair from twenty meters out.

"Hold the plane!" I shout. Her head snaps up from her computer. With no bag, no computer, and nothing to weigh me down, I close the distance at high school track runner's pace, although I can hardly stand when I get there.

"Oh honey," the woman says in a Texas drawl, "you just missed last call."

I nearly collapse, and feel tears jump to my eyes.

"Oh shucks, darlin', I'm just yankin' your chain. But you got about thirty seconds before that *is* true, so let me see your boardin' pass and if you don't chuck up a lung you can go ahead an get aboard."

I find my seat, a middle one. I pull out my phone and text her again, but there's no response. I text Franklin that I'm on the way but he doesn't respond either; he's likely asleep. I'll get in at two in morning. I remember that Franklin moved a few months back and I never got his new address, which means I'll need to sleep in the airport.

Once we're in the air and I settle into a seat that feels more like a city park bench than something designed for extended travel, I ask for a triple scotch. "We only do doubles," the long-faced, lisping flight attendant replies and I'm afraid that, if I try to bribe him or share my sob story, he'll punish me with none, so I just nod.

Twenty minutes into the flight my phone has died, and I'm left to flip through the in-flight magazine. The woman next to me snores; the man on the other side drools.

Three hours later I'm standing in LAX. I don't have clean clothes, toothbrush, or anything else; going to a hotel would be like replacing a bandage with the same bandage. So I find a couple of chairs in an out-of-the-way corner away from the TVs and, for what seems like hours, stare up at the ceiling.

I wake to the jarring roar of a vacuum. My back aches and my neck is torqued, but I lurch away from the groan of the machine, noticing only after a dozen steps that the sun has come up. I look around for a clock: 6:57. I find an open store, buy an iPhone charger, and sit on the floor next to an outlet. After a minute or two the phone comes to life. No messages. I lean my head back against the wall, watching legs and bags file past. My head hurts. I'm hungry. I look across the walkway at the restaurant that is opening and at the empty bar I know will be serving. I consider it. Twenty minutes passes and then my phone buzzes, snapping me out of a daze. My brother.

Yo. You in the City of Angels?? What's up, dog?

Hey. Some relationship trouble.

Oh? What kind?

Not in one anymore.

Ouch. Where are you?

Airport.

Get an Uber here.

Need the addy.

Ah. He sends it.

I have an 8am. Will not see you before you get in, and got a long day. You should hit up Alejandro. He's in Santa Monica. Only 10 miles away. He gets up early. Or goes to bed late.

Okay. See you tonight.

Key will be under mat. We'll go get a nice dinner and drinks. You can fill me in.

I look back at the bar, then text Alejandro.

Hey. In LA. At LAX actually.

The response is immediate: *Now?*

Yup.

You have plans?

No — Franklin is working.

I'll be there in 45 minutes or so. (LA.) In a powder blue Beetle. Convertible.

Of course you are.

☺ *Gate?*

Grab me in front of Spirit.

Oh honey. Discount air!

I get a Bloody Mary and some eggs and then go out into the California air. The sun feels like a stab and I realize I don't have sunglasses.

"Fuck," I mutter, shielding my face with my hand. I turn to head back inside when a powder blue Beetle appears with the top down and a bronze man inside. The car pulls up recklessly and Alejandro emerges from the driver's side. He has on white slacks and an off-white shirt, with matching low tops and no socks. Huge oval sunglasses cover much of his face, and his hair is still black and full even though he's at least in his mid-fifties. He looks trim and disciplined, like a former soldier or dancer, someone whose job was once to inhabit his body in a very particular way.

"Logan," he says formally, "you look like shit."

"Thanks, Alejandro."

"Where is your luggage?"

"I didn't bring any."

"Oh fuck. *That* kind of flight. That's why you're here at the crack of my ass." He looks over the tops of his sunglasses. "What was her name?"

But rather than laugh or say something smart I start to cry. Alejandro is surprised; for a moment he stands in front of me without moving as I put my face into my hand, but then he steps in and grabs me under each arm, hard, pulling me close. His arms, strong and sure, hold me and I give him most of my weight. I find myself weeping.

"*Shhhh,*" he soothes, "*shhhh* I'm sorry, Logan. I'm so sorry. You just hold on as long as you need," he whispers, which makes me cry even harder, ignoring the sunshine and the cars and the people all around us. I squeeze back, burying my face into his neck. I hold him for a long time, it seems, until the sobs that have taken control of me like seizures slow down. I feel a wave of embarrassment, and step away while wiping my face.

"I forgot my sunglasses," I say, stupidly, my voice sounding very young in my ears.

"Come," he says. He opens my door. "Glove box. Dolce and Gabbana." And there, in a case, are what must be three-hundred-dollar sunglasses, for when I put them on the world looks instantly cooler and more manageable.

He starts the car and pulls out a pack of cigarettes, lighting two and handing me one. "I know a place. Funky. Low key. Good Cuban food and great Cuban coffee. Generous cocktails. Let's go eat and you can tell me the long version of what happened." He looks over and, before pulling away, puts a hand on my shoulder for a moment, squeezing.

I turn away and more tears come from under the sunglasses as I look toward the door. Then I put my head back against the seat. The sun is warm on my face and the taste of the smoke is delightful in my mouth and, for the first time in as long as I can remember, I feel held.

Friday Night

Green-blue light eddies and flows on three walls of the enclosed bar and restaurant. Overhead a dark rectangle of night sky is framed and a few palm trees peer over the two-story interior enclosure. It's a narrow space, big enough to seat only twenty people, with a bar that faces a narrow pool from which the moving light emanates. It's a hipster bed and breakfast and restaurant, converted from a fifties motel that had, half a century before, been the cutting edge of kitsch.

"That was an amazing sunset," Alejandro comments. "So glad to have been able to spend it with the two of you." Sunglasses rest on top of his head.

"Sure as shit beats the East Coast," Franklin replies. "California wouldn't make any sense if it faced east. It can't. It's about letting go and starting over, but doing so in the not-so-sober light of the afternoon."

Alejandro chuckles. "New beginnings but not about the dawn. Cheers to that." They clink glasses and both look to me but I say nothing and leave my drink on the table. We have just finished a meal of steak frites and wine and are now getting cocktails.

"Oh honey," Alejandro sighs, "it's not as bad as all that." He smiles and his teeth, recently whitened, look like they were stolen from a teenager's mouth. His face is mostly unchanged by the passage of time, and the few lines he has are worn with distinction.

"You haven't aged," I note.

Alejandro lights a cigarette. "At thirty," he comments, looking at one of the arching palms and exhaling in that direction, "you have the face you're born with. By fifty you have the face you've earned."

"I feel vaguely insulted," Franklin smiles. "Logan, what's the name of the chick you had the affair with?" Sturdy denim and a black t-shirt give him an air of rockabilly reserve. My brother's blue eyes now match hair that's gone cool gray on top and snow white at the temples. Wrinkles around each eye respond to every smirk and smile and grimace, while a dusting of white stubble is blown across each cheek.

"Alea."

Alejandro follows, "Yeah — why don't you get together with that she-witch when you go back?"

"I texted her I wanted to spend more time with her," I say. "She sent me a message saying that I'm an amazing man — "

"Uh oh," Alejandro interjected.

"Yeah. An amazing man but that I should focus on feeling what's real for me and get clear on that before I get involved with another woman."

Alejandro and Franklin exchange a look.

"I've had weeks like that," Alejandro says with a sigh.

"I've had years like that," Franklin agrees.

"You talk to the ex-fiancée yet?" Alejandro asks. "It is ex now, right?"

I nod. "Definitely ex. She's pretty pissed off," I say, looking down at the poured concrete under my feet. "Not taking my calls."

"No doubt, and when she does talk to you, you're going to get an earful. I'm curious," Alejandro asks, "why you got engaged in the first place. Doesn't seem to fit you."

"I thought it was time to grow up. To let go of the dream of being a writer."

Alejandro takes a long, contemplative drag on his cigarette. "Let go of the dream?"

I nod.

"Why would you do that?"

I take a sip of my drink. "It's been a long time since I created anything worthwhile. I thought I'd try my hand at more conventional life." I look at my brother. "Remember when Jackson made fun of us, like a hundred years ago, for not taking straight jobs and just living out the American Dream, instead of trying to be artists?"

Franklin smiles. "That was the first of many times I endured that conversation."

"Yeah, and then you sort of took it in. You've retired from the dream of being a full time artist — and that hit me as a wakeup call." I look back to Alejandro. "It was a couple of things that told me it was time to grow up."

Alejandro gives me a lopsided grin. "Okay, but don't believe Franklin. He's full of shit."

Franklin smiles wryly.

"I moved to New York City in 1982," Alejandro says with a sigh. "But if you tell anyone that I'll kill you. I'd say 1992 but then my story wouldn't make any sense. Anyway, it was at what turned out to be the end of the last great identifiable art scene. I was just a pup, and an arrogant one at that."

A waiter comes to the table. "Bonjour," Alejandro says to the man.

"Salut. Comment allez-vous?"

"Tu parle français?"

"Évidemment oui."

Alejandro laughs and sits up. "I *love* the cultured. How many languages do you speak? Sprichst du Deutsch?"

"Ich spreche vier. Deutsch, na sicher. Français. Español."

"God," Alejandro says, "I thought only New York could offer this kind of thing. C'est fantastique." Alejandro orders a martini, up; Fanklin, a glass of wine; and me, a scotch.

"So," Alejandro continues, settling back. He lowers his sunglasses over his eyes, and in them I can see a funhouse version of myself, the blue-green pool, and the bar. "I ended up getting to know the most famous artists of the day; I was convinced that I was one of them, of course, even though I was just out of school and barely had a portfolio together. I was at a cocktail party and I ran into Basquiat." Alejandro pauses. "You know who he is?"

Franklin leans away from us, his attention drawn toward the bar, his eyes on a lean brunette who's just walked up to it.

"Of course."

"Good boy. So I meet him at a party. We were both wasted. He was on heroin and I was on coke, which is to say I talked and he listened."

Franklin laughs.

"It was the good old days, before the acronyms ruined everything."

I take the bait. "The acronyms?"

"AIDS. MADD. HIV. AA. NA. So Basquiat. What a beautiful boy. I was a boy, too, but he was so lean and so black and so beautiful. My god. He had a masterful mind and dashing technique — one of the true, and only, geniuses to rise out of Warhol's narcissism camp. How I wanted to be a part of that camp; I was arrogant and gay enough, God knows. Anyway, we were wasted, and I showed him my portfolio."

"I'll be right back," Franklin says, heading toward the bar.

Alejandro glances over for a moment, watching him walk away. "So, Basquiat. This beautiful tortured boy with this kinky hair and deep eyes. We're on a couch, in the apartment of some curator, some queen with awful taste who was into floral paintings. Terrible. Basquiat flips through a few pages of my book, and closes it about a quarter of the way through. 'Okay,' he says. He had this soft voice, a high pitch, and he stuttered over his words. 'It's, it's, it's fine, man.' And he hands my book back to me."

"But I wasn't having any of that. I wanted him to *validate* my work." Alejandro shakes his head. "So I pressed him. *How* was it fine, *what* did he like about it, stuff like that. But he's all whacked out on heroin, so he's sort of speaking through this distant fog. 'You could be a, a, a, a pro,' he says, 'but you're all technique, man. No, no, no *heart*.'"

Alejandro takes a sip of his drink, and I look at myself looking at him in his oversized sunglasses. "His eyes weren't on me, but instead kind of up at the ceiling. Then he looks over. He says: 'This is just some shit to hang on a wall.'"

"Holy crap. What did you say?"

Alejandro's tone goes up an octave. "I thought he was being a cunt. I huffed off. After all, I saw us as *equals*." He pauses, glancing over at Franklin, who is talking to the brunette.

"You're a writer, Logan. An *artist*, who is, what did you say to us earlier today, *standing in the ruins of his own life*? So do you know the moral of the story?"

I run a hand through my hair. "An artist? My novel came out years ago. Now I'm just a guy trying to survive."

I watch his expressionless face consider that. "Now," he says, a groomed eyebrow appearing over the top of his sunglasses, "you're being either falsely modest or defensive. Neither of which is very attractive, or very smart."

I feel my temper flare momentarily.

"Oh," Alejandro says, "some fire is in there after all." At that moment Franklin comes back to the table and sits down quietly.

"You get her number?" Alejandro doesn't look at him.

Franklin merely smiles.

"*Whore*. I was an arrogant little fuck who believed too strongly in himself. That's a mistake. It means when a genius like Basquiat tells you something that could change the course of your life, you listen. He was right, of course. My work was all technique and sense of entitlement. His was all passion and inspiration. He didn't give a fuck about recognition or fame." Alejandro grinds out his cigarette. "You?" He exhales out the side of his mouth. "You're a falsely modest man but I *know* you believe in yourself, or you wouldn't be in the pain you're in.

The *kind* of pain you're in. *Enduring* what you're enduring, and speaking about things in such — " his hand makes a large gesture " — *grand* terms. Affairs and the end of relationships are pedestrian, after all, as common and as interesting as bad breath. But I can see the pain in your eyes. You wear it like a cheap suit."

I look at Alejandro coldly and feel my face flush in anger, but he scoffs. "And proud and obvious in your outrage too. *Please.* It doesn't fit you well. It tells me, in fact, that you're more vested in this than you want to admit." He looks to Franklin. "I don't mean to be a cunt, but it's just someone needs to tell him straight."

Franklin nods.

Alejandro takes off his sunglasses and sets them on the table, his eyes moist and tender and very white. "I won't pity you, honey — I care too much. Your fiancée died, and it was a tragedy. I knew Carissa. My heart breaks for you." He pauses and glances at Franklin.

"*And* it was a lifetime ago. So you had an affair because you were in a shit relationship and took a shit job you should have never taken and were drowning in middle-aged white depression and you needed to feel what it was like to burn like an acetylene torch again. What it was like to live like an artist again, balls out, fuck all to the world. You're not an arrogant little prick like I was, but you're making the opposite mistake, being falsely humble and pretending you don't have something important to share. Because they're really the same thing, don't you see, the arrogance and the modesty? They're both about fear."

I sit back as our drinks arrive with our multilingual waiter. He and Alejandro exchange some pleasantries in German as I look off to the bar. When the waiter leaves I feel Franklin's and Alejandro's eyes on me.

"If my dreams stood before me as years, I would live forever," I say, barely above a whisper.

Alejandro nods. "And look at yourself," he gestures up and down with his right hand. "Despite your obvious shock, you look lighter than you've been in twenty years. Despite all that's happened."

"Because of it," Franklin says.

Alejandro nods in agreement. "You look *free*."

"I was convinced," says Franklin, "that I was going to be the next Picasso. That if I worked hard enough, the skies would open and champagne would spill from the sky, especially after all those solo shows, the press, the museums, the huge freelance jobs, all the signs that said it was happening. Year after year after year I danced on the cusp of fame, the cusp of breaking through. Now you can be famous for your Instagram feed. Why bother with all that creation and rejection when a big part of what we wanted — fame and money — can be had without any of the risk?"

"Because it's not about the fame or money," Alejandro counters, but Franklin just shakes his head, his right foot tapping quickly.

"Of course that's what it's about. Obscurity is hell for an artist, the same as not creating. I work a full time job now," he says. "I am a fucking worker bee. I have some shows now and again. It's enough. I don't need to be the known artist anymore. I don't care about that shit anymore."

Alejandro shakes his head. "Yes you do. Same as me."

Franklin's voice rises. "Hey man, you want to keep living the artist's dream and stay inside that purgatory, that's on you. Don't drag me into it." The wrinkles around his eyes and mouth deepen in sympathy and the tapping of his foot increases its tempo.

Alejandro puts his sunglasses back on top of his head. "I haven't given up," he retorts. "I still paint. I still have exhibitions. I still shoot." He looks at both of us. "I still hope that one day ... " But he stops and, to my great surprise, tears come to his eyes. He blinks them away while looking to the bar but otherwise doesn't try to hide his face. Then those dark eyes come back to us. "Yeah," he says with a hollow laugh, "I still hope."

"I don't," Franklin says. "I can't believe you have the energy for it. Just do the work for yourself, man, like you said about Basquiat. The days of making a living from art are behind us, and maybe that's not a bad thing. Today everyone's an artist. Everyone's a writer. Everyone's a fucking genius. Jackson was right when he told us to just get a job and be happy with that. He's retiring in a couple of years, and we're all still stuck inside the grind, even without kids."

"It wasn't about the fame and money," I say finally, and both look to me. "It was about the freedom to express myself, the dizziness of knowing that what came out of my head might entertain and inspire people."

There's music flowing through the air and I can hear the sounds of traffic spilling in from the street. For a moment I feel warm and safe tucked inside the blue-green womb of the bar. Alejandro is looking off into the distance.

"I wish," Alejandro says, "it was just as simple as doing what we love, living our dream with hard work and vision. Not doing that has such huge cost, like a piece of our soul is dying." He smiles sadly. "And the same thing happens when you do it." He looks at Franklin, who doesn't meet his gaze but instead stands and drains his drink in a single gulp. His silver belt buckle reflects the lights of the pool back to us and his face is a mask of control.

"Let's get out of here. I'm over this place," my brother says.

"Where's next?" asks Alejandro.

"Anywhere but here."

Monday

After a few more days in Los Angeles, I book a ticket to New York City and rent a room off Airbnb, not far from my old neighborhood. The days are cold and dark, with a low sky crowding in not much higher than the tops of some of the buildings. I spend my time wandering the streets of the East Village, seeing the ghosts of Carissa and Logan, who still laugh and smile and hold hands.

I walk across the Brooklyn Bridge and rest there, taking in the full potential of New York as it rises over the waters of the Hudson. Without the World Trade Center, the skyline is different from the one I remember but it no longer looks like something is missing. It is, instead, regal and grand, fully itself, even if it's no longer mine.

For an hour or more I watch the throngs of people walk past me on the bridge. I then wander down to the Empire Fulton Ferry State Park to sit on the frozen grass in the lengthening shadows of the day. Off the southern tip of the island, small in the distance, stands the Statue of Liberty, an homage to those brave enough to follow their dreams across an ocean. Sitting there, it is easy for me to remember that once, if you had been willing to endure hardship for the chance of something bigger, you might have found yourself staring up at the unapologetic hugeness of New York, the gateway to a new world.

Maybe New York was the last great place that could loom larger even than the dreams that brought people to her. The city represented the vastness of hope itself, something deeper than reason, unbound by fear and larger even than love, for it was hope that fired the imagination of the heart.

Postscript

Monday was to be my last day in New York, but I've been writing and editing all of this over the past few weeks. I'm still in the city, staying not far from where Carissa and I once lived. It's only now, as I'm reading over these stories, that the patterns of my life emerge out of their seeming randomness. While I would normally be thinking I was once again standing at a crossroads, I see the idea I've lived with — that I have to choose a path, that there is one way to go at the cost of the other — is the idea that has plagued me. Life isn't so neat as to offer clear paths like distinct quanta; it unfolds messily in all directions all at once and we impose a narrative and an order on something that is inherently chaotic. I see, now, as Sylvie pointed out so many years ago, that it's not unreasonable for me to have loved a woman with all my heart, even though she has been dead for nearly a dozen years, nor unreasonable that I was blinded to that love by the depth of my pain.

Only my dreams remain pregnant with the possibility that I might see Carissa again. In some of them I'm young and I'll be somewhere — a coffee shop, a mall, walking through a park — and I'll catch sight of her and feel relief that the heartache was just imagined. And some nights she turns and greets me and we laugh and joke, or I cry and she holds me and whispers apologies for having been gone so long. It's hard to awaken from those dreams, to know the dull throb of heartache, suddenly acute, is the real world and that she's left me once more.

The Airbnb I'm renting has a gas fireplace and a deck where I can sit for an hour or two in the afternoon sun. The kitchen area has brick along one wall and lots of natural lighting. This is where I'm sitting now, in the later morning on a bitterly cold December day. I've bought new clothes and other things I need to live for awhile here, even though it's mostly on credit and borrowed time.

This morning she called. We haven't spoken since the night I left Colorado.

"Hey," I said, trying to sound like I was already up and that my heart wasn't pounding.

"Hey," she replied, unguarded.

A few heartbeats, a nervous silence as we both listened for the other.

"You know it's over," she said, speaking first.

"Yes." An exhale. "I think it's been over for awhile. Maybe neither one of us wanted to admit it."

"Maybe. Why did you do it?"

I rolled onto my back and looked up at the popcorn ceiling. A gray light illuminated the edges of the curtains and I wondered if it was going to be another forlorn day.

"I don't know. It was nothing you did. I think maybe your vision — the kids and the marriage and all of that — seemed to offer me benediction from my own past, a way to let go of the broken dreams and the broken heart and start fresh."

"Only there's no starting fresh."

I nodded to the room. "There's no starting fresh," I repeated. "We bring our ghosts with us no matter where we go."

She was quiet. "Until we set them free."

"Is it pointless to say I'm sorry?"

"It's never pointless."

"I am. Sorry." I had started to cry, and she waited quietly for me to gather myself.

"I know," she said, gently. "And I don't want to hate you. But I do need space. From you. To heal."

"I understand."

"I had movers come and pack up all your things and take them to storage. I'll email you the bill and the address and key code."

"Okay."

"Your computer is with that stuff."

"Okay."

She considered that. "Don't you need it?"

"Franklin had an old Mac I'm borrowing and all the files I need are in Dropbox."

"Oh." She paused. "When are you coming back?"

"I don't know."

A siren in the background.

"Where are you?"

"The East Village."

I could almost hear the nod. "Where it all started for you. And, I think, where it all has to end." She sighed. "I hope you find what you need there."

I said nothing.

"Be good to yourself, Logan."

"I'll do my best. You too."

The line went dead and I stayed in bed another ten minutes, feeling the sensations that went through me: relief, regret, anger, anxiety, shame. Then I got up, made coffee, and sat down to write an end to ... whatever this is.

And now, outside, the dark morning has turned into a grey afternoon. No more forks in my road, no more false binaries, no more this or that. Just life arising in all of its perfect imperfection. And I've realized something. Carissa is with me, a part of me, indivisible. And while I miss her laugh and her smile, her enormous heart and her wit, I see her reflected in all that I do and am. And there's solace in that, for I don't need to let go of something that is a part of me — I just need to be willing to feel it. If this were a work of philosophy or great literature, it would wind itself down in worded eloquence, providing a lasting lesson about life and love, truth or art. But it's not. It's just life.

###

Special Thanks

A novel takes many hands to create beyond merely the artist's. This book came into view over four long years of transformation and challenge, collapse and acceptance, and ultimately inspiration and support.

For those who used Kickstarted to provide financial backing to allow me the free time to create, I especially want to thank the Integral Center, Maria Bailey, Johnny Jenkins, Darrin Wilson, William Frates, the late Mark Resnick, Melissa Zeligman, Eric Altman, and Robert McNaughton.

Additionally, Kathryn Thomas provided indispensable assistance as my editor, helping me to get out of my own way.

Many people inspired the characters and scenes in this book, though none are meant to be an accurate or honest reflection of anyone I know.

About the Author

Keith Martin-Smith has a passion for the untold stories that drive us, the things that push us to grow and question our world and ourselves.

Only Everything is Keith's fourth book and first novel. A collection of short stories, *The Mysterious Divination of Tea Leaves,* was published in 2009, followed in 2012 by the award-winning memoir *A Heart Blown Open* and its follow-up, *The Heart of Zen.*

In addition to being an author, Keith is also an ordained Zen priest and a Northern Kung Fu lineage holder and recognized master. But just so you don't get the wrong idea, he's also fond of sleeping in and drinking ales.

More on Keith at www.keithmartinsmith.com

CPSIA information can be obtained
at www.ICGtesting.com
Printed in the USA
FSHW01n2243260718
50895FS